STORY TELLING FORTY ONE

The Petite Chronicles

By Trudie Le Beau

Story Telling is proud to introduce the accomplished and skilful writings of Trudie Le Beau.

We present a collection of totally different short stories all unique and difficult to guess the ending

Unique & Different

The Petite Chronicles

In this busy world I hope the reader will enjoy this collection of short stories which for the most part are just the right length to enjoy with a coffee break.

My thanks go to my family for supporting and encouraging me in my endeavours.

Trudie Le Beau

June 2020

Previous Published novels by Trudie

The Throgmorton Legacy
White Gold
A Debt Repaid

The Petite Chronicles

Published by

Percychatteybooks Publishing

ISBN 978 1 9162712 8 9

Copyright Trudie Le Beau 2020

The Petite Chronicles

By Trudie Le Beau

Content

Journey Untaken

Mary Finlay and her husband Donald bowed their heads against the driving rain that stung their faces as they made their way slowly to Wormit station, with Donald all the while making clicking noises and calling out to calm their old Mare Chestnut who had become unsettled by the sudden deterioration in the weather. Mary clutched the precious rail ticket in her pocket hardly able to contain her excitement at the thought of meeting her eldest daughter Moira, even if it was for only one day.

Moira was in service in Dundee, and although her employers were kindly they had refused her permission to visit her parents over Christmas, although they were more than happy for her to receive a visit from her mother once the festivities were over so, because he loved his wife so much, Donald had spent a reasonable amount of their savings on the rail fare, and although he'd had a few misgivings about spending the money, they all disappeared when he saw the joy on his beloved wife's face as he handed over her ticket.

Soaked to the skin, they reached the station and Mary jumped down to retrieve her small overnight bag, now holding her ticket in her hand in readiness for her trip, but as she reached out for the bag she was nearly blasted off her feet by a gust of wind that caused Chestnut to rear up dragging the trap a few yards along the road. Fearing for Donald who had fallen backwards from his bench seat,

Mary rushed forward arms outstretched so that she could catch the reins and hold the horse until Donald was back in control.

She shouted above the wind "You go home now Donald and quickly before it gets dark, a storm is building and I don't want you out in it."

Mary grabbed his face and pulled him towards her kissing him on the lips, "Go on now. I'll be fine in the shelter of the station and I'll be back the day after tomorrow when I can tell you all about how Moira is getting on." She turned hurrying toward the small station, but stopped dead in her tracks crying out "Oh no, oh no!"

Donald jumped down from the trap "What is it Mary, are you hurt?"

"My ticket; where is my ticket? It was in my hand and now………………."

Realisation dawned and they began a futile search for the small piece of card, fighting the howling wind and freezing rain which was now beating down on them, but to no avail – the ticket was gone. Mary fell to her knees in despair before Donald helped her up and into the station where they pleaded with the station manager to let Mary take the train but he stood firm, "No ticket, no journey."

Beaten, they turned for home but the storm reached such a pitch that they had to take shelter through the worst of it and it was almost daylight when, saddened beyond belief they reached their little cottage and by now very worried children. Mary went inside to comfort her brood whilst Donald saw to old Chestnut. He fed her and lay out fresh dry straw, "I'm so sorry we had to take you out in that old girl – and all for nothing too." He sighed and weary to the bone he walked into the cottage.

Although Hogmanay was something that usually lifted the spirits in the Finlay household, this year it was tinged with sadness. Mary still went through the motions of preparation but really her heart wasn't in it. She felt so sad that poor Moira would think she had let her down, and guilty because she knew Donald had spent money they could ill afford on her ticket and she had been so foolish as to lose it.

She was just reaching over the fire for a kettle of hot water when Donald burst in and gathered her into his arms, holding her so tight that she could hardly breathe. "Donald, whatever is the matter. Is it old Chestnut is she poorly from the other night?"

Reluctantly Donald released her from his grip. "I'm just thanking The Lord for sparing you my love." Mary didn't understand but when she went to speak he put up his hand to silence her, "That night, in the storm, when you lost your ticket."

Mary nodded her head "Yes dear, how could I ever forget it?"

"That night Mary, the new bridge collapsed. The train went into the Tay and everyone on it is dead."

His words rang around the room bouncing into her ears, but not making any sense. Gradually she was able to absorb the meaning of them, shuddering when they hit home. She reached for her husband who wrapped his arms around her kissing her forehead and there they stayed clinging to each other, both now rejoicing the loss of the ticket which had resulted in her journey not being taken and, as a consequence, nor had she.

Authors Note: *The newly constructed Tay Bridge, which was opened to the public in 1878, collapsed in stormy weather on 28th December 1879 plunging a train and 75 passengers and crew into the river Tay – there were no survivors.*

Ada's Law

November 25th 8.30pm

Inspector Nick Murray put down the phone "We've got another one Josh."

Sergeant Josh McGiven looked quizzically at his superior "Another what Gov?"

Another body, one shot to the body and one to the head and I'm guessing

the bullets will be 22 caliber just like the others. Someone called it in from the Shedwell Estate and our local lad was on the scene almost immediately – reckons this one can't have been dead more than an hour."

Josh leant back in his chair with his hands behind his head, "That makes six in the last nine months and we've got no idea who's doing it, or why! They look like gang related executions but so far none of the victims fit that kind of picture." He grabbed his jacket from the back of his seat, "Typical, it's pissing down and we've got to get soaked because there's some maniac roaming around pretending to be John Wayne."

"You could have something there Josh. Maybe there is some crazy vigilante out there punishing these men, but for the life of me I can't see any connection between them – maybe this one will give us a clue."

Two weeks earlier

The Shedwell Estate was a run-down collection of miserable looking concrete monoliths that housed what society tended to call 'problem families,' and that looked more like a prison camp than a housing estate. The roads surrounding it had been narrowed by concrete blocks in order to stop joy riding and speed humps proliferated. The one good thing in it's favour was that it was surrounded by fields and common ground and was therefore a popular spot for joggers and dog walkers.

Ada walked Bobby there quite regularly and on this particular November afternoon, as she was returning to her car, she heard raised voices and then a woman screaming. As she was putting her key in the lock a woman came running towards her sobbing and clutching her head and not being able to see through her tears, she collided with Ada. It looked to Ada as though she had been punched on the nose, and pretty hard at that as one of her eyes was beginning to swell. She was sobbing uncontrollably and shivering violently. Her coat was undone and Ada could see that she had scant clothing underneath it – she obviously left home in a hurry.

"Whatever is the matter my dear? You'll catch your death out here dressed like that." She unlocked her car, "Here, come on sit inside with me for a while. I'll start the engine and get the heater going." The young woman did not resist and let Ada guide her into the passenger seat. Ada grabbed Bobby's rug from the back seat and wrapped it around her, "Now who did this to you – can I take you to the police station?"

"No, no. I'll be alright. You're very kind – whatever must you think of me I..."

"I'm thinking that somebody has hit you and," she'd noticed the marks on the woman's arms, "I'm guessing that it's not for the first time."

"He doesn't mean it. I just annoy him. He's lovely really – he's just frustrated 'cos he can't get a job and....."

"I know, I know, it's not his fault it's yours."

The woman began to sob again, "I'd better go back – my little boy will wonder where I've gone. He'll be frightened." She pushed down the rug and began to fasten her coat.

"Why do you stay with him?"

The woman wiped her eyes on the handkerchief that Ada had offered, "Because I love him."

Ada sighed and shook her head "They all say that."

A rough looking man appeared and started walking purposefully toward them. At the sight of him the woman started and opened the car door, fear written all over her face, "I've got to go but thank you."

"Wait, what's your name?"

"Julie, it's Julie. Please go – he doesn't like me talking to people," and with that she was off.

Ada watched as the couple met and the man put his arm around his woman, ruffling her hair. She started the car and looked at Bobby in the rear view mirror, "It's all honkey dory now, eh Bobby – until the next time that is."

On her regular walks with Bobby Ada kept an eye out for Julie but although there were plenty of young women pushing tots in prams none of them were her. A couple of weeks went by and one afternoon on a whim she called into the local supermarket on her way home from dog walking and virtually bumped into her. If anything Julie looked worse than before. Her swollen eye had receded but her top lip was badly swollen, and her arm was in a sling. "Hello dear. Oh my, what happened to you?" Julie made a half hearted excuse about falling down but they both knew the truth behind her injuries.

"Why don't you let me buy you a coffee dear and ..."

"No, no. I've got to go, he doesn't like me being too long. He's waiting in the car park. See you sometime," and with that she was gone.

....

As Ada sat by the fire that evening sipping her port and lemon she pondered on the ways of the world. Her mind drifted back to her own childhood and her own unbending cruel father who had ruled his little kingdom with a rod of iron, beating her mother up whenever he was 'in a temper'. As a consequence Ada and her younger brother Sid had left home at the earliest opportunity. They both regretted leaving their mother with such a brutal man, but although they tried hard to persuade her she would not leave him and had unselfishly encouraged them to get away and 'make their way in the world'.

She had enlisted in the WRACS at the earliest opportunity and her career in the army had taken her to places where she had witnessed the abysmal lives that so many women in the world were subjected to. She had developed an abiding hatred of the cruelty and injustice meted out to them by men just because they could. It had struck a chord with her, reviving memories that she had tried so hard to forget and reinforcing her conviction that men were not to be trusted and to be avoided where possible.

Consequently, she was well beyond the first flush of youth when she'd met Stan. He was a career soldier whose first wife, not being suited to army life, had divorced him. The friendship that had developed from the occasional social meetings had caught them both by surprise and after several months they had to admit that they were in love. They were married and had nearly twenty seven blissful years together before Stan lost his battle with illness leaving Ada alone and inconsolable. She sipped her port and stroked Bobby's head as she remembered those dreadful days so thankful of the dog's existence.

She thought back to the day that Stan had come home with the Beretta. The situation around their posting abroad had become uncertain and things seemed to be taking a turn for the worse. Stan dismissed any questions she had as to how he had obtained the gun, only saying that he was worried about her safety and he'd got it 'just in case'. That night she had been given a tutorial on how to take it apart, load and clean it and the next day he had taken her to a deserted area to show her how to use it.

Eventually they had retired to the terraced house in the leafy suburb in which she still lived, and the gun had come with them. Occasionally Stan would take it out to clean and oil it, understanding her feminism and knowing how strongly she felt about men who abused their position. Stan had often joked about her using it. "There you are Ada. If anyone gets on your nerves just get 'em down a blind alley and pop 'em off – tell 'em you're administering Ada's Law."

She poured another drink and sighed deeply. He'd laughed at his joke – she wondered what he would think about her now.

November 25th 6.00pm

Ada turned off the gas under her stew, told Bobby to be a good boy while she was out and, after checking for the umpteenth time that her auburn wig and loaded Beretta were in her shopping bag, drove off her forecourt into light traffic. It was a chill night but not as cold as it could be in November and she was glad of that. She stopped a couple of streets away and pulled on her wig, making minor adjustments in her rear view mirror and once satisfied she drove off once more. Her eventual destination was the Shedwell Estate but she chose to park a good ten minutes walk away close to a large block of flats on the basis that it was a busy thoroughfare and neither she nor her car would be likely to lodge in anyone's memory. She fitted her crook lock then began to make her way to the vantage point she had chosen.

She knew from earlier observations that her target was in the habit of spending most of his evening in The Queens Head, and she knew that rather than walk along the streets, he preferred to take the short cut across rough ground that separated the estate from his watering hole. She nestled as best she could into the small group of gorse bushes near the entrance to the rough path and waited hoping that he would appear. She was getting too old to be standing around in the cold and of course there was always the possibility that he would choose to stay in the warm himself.

The main entrance to the Estate was well lit so she had a good view of anyone entering or leaving. She must have been waiting for at least half an hour, although it felt much longer and she was just about to give up and go home, when she spotted a man walking in her direction. As he passed under one of the street lights her heart skipped a beat – it was him!

She took off her gloves and reached into her bag taking out the gun and slipping it into her coat pocket. She looked all around and listened but there seemed to be no-one else around. When her quarry was a few metres away she stepped onto the path and feigned distress. "Oh please help me. I seem to have lost my way, " she made up a name, "I'm looking for Queens Road – do know it?"

The man peered into the gloom annoyed with the silly old bat, "Never 'eard of it. Go and ask a police.."

Ada took the gun from her pocket, aimed and fired hitting her target square in the chest. As he lay on the ground she bent over him and shot him once more in the head. "Belt and braces Ada – belt and braces." Heart thumping she stood still listening hard - all was quiet thank The Lord. Slipping the gun back into her bag she retraced her steps trying not to hurry, listening all the while for chasing footsteps.

Once back in her car she felt a little safer. Her hands were trembling which made it hard to deal with the crook lock so she forced herself to just sit back and listen to the radio for ten minutes until she had regained some control. The last thing she wanted was to be involved in some sort of accident. Gradually she calmed down and was able to release the lock on the wheel. She switched on the wipers to clear the screen as it had now begun to rain and after a few more minutes she set off for home.

She began to relax as she neared her house she slipped off the wig as she drove, a few minutes later she was thankful to be pulling onto her forecourt safe and sound. She pushed her car door too hoping that none of her neighbours had noticed her brief absence then let herself in where she received a rapturous greeting from Bobby. Once all was calm she hid the bag containing the gun and wig in her secret place and made her way into the kitchen.

"Now then Bobby let's see about something to eat shall we?" She heated up the stew she'd made earlier and prepared Bobby's dinner. She ladled the steaming stew into one bowl for her and put it on a tray alongside the dog's bowl then carried it into her lounge. She put the tray onto a nest of tables that sat beside her favourite armchair. "There we are then Bobby", she put his bowl down onto his feeding mat then picked up the television remote as she plumped up the cushions and settled into her seat, "Now let's enjoy our meals and see if there's anything worth watching on the tele."

Ageing

Almost from the beginning of civilisation man has searched for the elixir of life but to no avail. Old father time moves inexorably on taking us with him, albeit reluctantly, and despite the plethora of creams and lotions, all of which claim to work miracles and defy ageing, and most of which I have slapped on with a vengeance, I have experienced no such miracles and have had to resignedly observe the onset of sagging skin, wrinkles and developing jowls knowing that these changes are inevitable and go with the territory when one enters the realms of the more mature.

Nowadays of course there is the option of employing a skilled surgeon to eliminate these tell tale signs of one's age, but this cannot happen without money, and sometimes a great deal of it, changing hands, so the realms of plastic surgery are for the most part peopled only by the rich and famous and are not an option for Mr and Mrs average.

In many ways though there is a down side for those fortunate few, as it is now so common to see seventy year olds with lips like cod fish, or looking as though they have just been stuck in a wind tunnel, that having 'procedures' has almost become a necessary evil – almost like keeping up with the Joneses. In those circles it just isn't done any more to age, either gracefully or otherwise.

I saw Goldie Hawn on the television last year and just didn't recognise her. I thought I recognised her voice but until her name was mentioned I just couldn't be sure. As it happens she looked very nice, although her smooth young looking face and barbie-doll hair looked a bit at odds with her obviously aged hands, but at least I suppose you could say her 'procedures' had been a success. It needs to be borne in mind though that unfortunately things do go drastically wrong for some poor folk, and I think we've all seen the odd example of that, so on the whole I would say that the age defying thing is a lottery to be steered clear of – and that isn't sour grapes of course – really!.

My take on getting old is to be grateful. Yes, like everyone else I get aches and pains and I'm considerably slower in mind and body than I was, and yes, it is sad sometimes to look through old photos and see a younger smooth faced version of myself, but that's a luxury many of the friends and family that I have lost over the years never had, so I think I'll just slide gracefully into my dotage and regard my wrinkles as a badge of honour, a reward for long service and surely the precious years I have left are my very own golden handshake.

BITTER SWEET

Bette sat contemplating her surroundings as the smell of soon to be served lunch wafted through the building. Her little apartment was very comfortable with a living room which she had been allowed to furnish herself, a small kitchenette should she wish to exercise her culinary independence, and a small bedroom and shower room discreetly placed behind a partition.

She tried to count her blessings and always look at the positives in her life, but today she was tired and allowed her mind to ponder on the events of the past few months, and despite her best efforts she began to sob.

She and her husband Bob had been so happy together. They had worked hard and eventually bought a small house then upgraded over the years until they had moved into a bungalow overlooking the sea – their dream home. Their lives were made complete when, well after they had given up all hope of having a child, Bette had discovered that she was pregnant and had eventually given birth to their son, Steven.

Because they loved him so they had of course over indulged the boy and as a result his teenage years had been nothing but purgatory. So many times he had hurt Bob with his taunts and insults whenever he was denied even the smallest thing. He was an exceptionally clever boy and did well getting a first at Cambridge University no less, but there was no thanks forthcoming for their efforts to keep him there, just a haughty contempt for everything in life that they represented, although they were good enough for him and Cherie, his newly acquired girl friend, to live off for the few months that it took him to get a job.

So that was how it had been over the years. No real contact, just the occasional visit when and if they happened to be in the area. She still vividly remembered the fateful day they arrived out of the blue and for once Seven was uncharacteristically attentive and actually agreed to stay for tea instead of rushing off after the usual perfunctory half hour. It was all very convivial until Steven mentioned that they were looking for a loan as he had seen a piece of land and wanted to build a small block of flats on it. He had done his research and had their bungalow valued explaining that if they sold he could afford to buy the land and build, and almost as an afterthought he sweetened the pill by saying that she and Bob could have whichever of the completed flats they would like.

This was just too much for Bob who had snapped and thrown them out. Their son had broken his heart and he was never the same after that. He grew old before her eyes and seemed to lose interest in their beautiful home. Up until that time he was always hustling and bustling around, re-arranging the garden, pricing up conservatories, poring over paint samples, but from that day he did nothing but sometimes take himself off for solitary walks – he had given up on life. She clenched her hands in her lap; she blamed her own son for his father's death. Her darling Bob, oh how she missed him so.

She had been so lonely without Bob that she had resumed writing – something which had always given her great comfort as she could immerse herself in some other life and as she was in control, never be disappointed with the outcome. She had even sent off a few manuscripts but as expected the replies from those who had bothered had been along the lines of "thanks – but no thanks."

There was a knock on the door and Matron's head appeared. "Lunch will be ready in twenty minutes Bette – Chicken casserole today and fresh strawberries and cream."

"Lovely, I'll be along shortly."

The door closed and Bette went back to her thoughts. She had carried on as best she could on her own until two years ago when she caught the flu. Probably because she had neglected herself a little she had been unable to shake it off and was taken to hospital after collapsing with pneumonia. Apparently she had been close to death's door and pretty ill for several weeks and during that time Steven had come to visit. He had been so caring and asked her to sign papers giving access to her bank accounts as she would need to convalesce for a while and he wanted only the best for her. It would be expensive but she was all he had left and if necessary he would help out with the fees. She had been so touched by his concern and in her feeble state had been so grateful that he cared.

Although quite a way from her home in Torquay, The Retreat was indeed a beautiful place. Steven came to settle her in. "Only the best for you Mum. After all, you can't take it with you so just enjoy being waited on for once." He kissed her forehead "I'll be back soon but in the meantime just you get back to your old self."

Steven didn't come back. After several weeks she stopped looking out of the window every time she heard a car crunching its' way up the drive. She was feeling fine now and began to think clearly, this place was costing her a fortune so the sooner she left the better. She dressed and made her way to Matron's office knocking gently as she opened the door.

"Ah, Bette; I was just on my way to see you. We have a couple of issued that need clearing up and....."

"If it's about the hairdresser, I'll pay her today, but I've just come to tell you that I am feeling so much better now and I think it's time I went home."

Matron looked confused. "Well, what do you mean dear? You are a permanent resident here and that's what I need to speak to you about."

A cold shaft of fear pierced Bette's heart. "No, I just came to convalesce, but like I just said, I'm fine now and I'm going home."

Matron shifted uncomfortably in her chair. "We seem to be talking at cross purposes dear." She put up a hand as Bette jumped up from her seat, "Let's start at the beginning shall we?"

Bette was beginning to panic "Don't talk to me as though I'm an idiot. I am going home and that's the end of it."

"But I don't think you have a home to go to dear, and while we are on the subject your fees have not been paid for the last three weeks. Your son assured me he would set up a direct debit but I'm afraid he hasn't done so and we have been unable to contact him. The telephone number he gave us ......"

Bette's head was spinning "I am so sorry Matron, I had no idea the fees weren't being paid; when I get home I'll arrange a transfer for whatever is outstanding. I can't understand what can have happened to Steven."

Matron was full of compassion, she stood and put a hand on Bette's shoulder. "I don't think you understand fully my dear, let me explain, but first," she picked up the direct line to the kitchen and ordered two coffees and one brandy, "Now Bette, when your son came to view The Retreat he said that he had Power of Attorney and that your fees would be met from the proceeds of your house sale which was just about to complete. So you see, your house has been sold – you have no home to go to." The two coffees arrived and Matron tipped the brandy and two sugars into one and held it out for Bette. "Sip this now dear and we'll try to unravel what appears to be quite a mess."

It was a mess indeed. It transpired that Bette's bank accounts had been shut down and agents in Torquay confirmed that her home had been sold so she was in effect homeless and penniless apart from the two hundred pounds that Steven had so thoughtfully insisted she keep in her purse for any little extras. Staff at The Retreat, particularly Carlotta one of the carers, had rallied round and made a small collection for her and Matron had sorted out the council accommodation in Torquay that she now called home. The fees for the estate agents and the nursing home were still outstanding and Bette had never felt so angry and ashamed. She thanked God that Bob had not lived to see how his son had turned out and she felt nothing for her own flesh and blood but contempt and hatred.

She patted her eyes and sighed deeply, that had all been nearly two years ago now, but it still hurt to her very core. She had revoked the Power of Attorney and mentally cast her son into the abyss. A knock on the door cleared her mind and her dear friend Charlie walked in and held out an arm. "Would you like to accompany me to luncheon my dear?"

She punched his arm "You are a fool Charlie – it´s chicken casserole today." She slipped her arm through his, "Lead on McDuff."

She had made many friends since coming to The Briars but Charlie had been a life saver. Although he hadn't owned his own home his daughter had treated him pretty badly and he, like her, had finished up feeling lonely and unloved, cast off like an old shoe. They had immediately formed a bond, understanding more than most how it felt to be wounded by one's own children.

They had a very pleasant lunch followed by a sing song lead by Aggie – she had been an entertainer in her youth and proved to be a tonic that boosted moral at The Briars and her effervescent nature was much appreciated by both staff and residents.

They were just walking back to Bette's room when someone called out her name. Bette turned to see dear Carlotta hurrying down the corridor all smiles and with arms outstretched. Bette hugged her tightly. "Oh my dear how lovely it is to see you, and you look so well."

Carlotta smiled and fanned her flushed face as she cast an eye over Charlie. Bette made the introductions and they continued on to her rooms where she put on the kettle and poured out three sherries. As she handed them round Carlotta explained that she had brought some mail. Steven had re-directed her mail to his own house but some still got through and the new owners of her bungalow posted it on to her believing that she was still at The Retreat.

There were three letters, one from The Heart Foundation wondering if she would like to renew her subscription, one regarding a quotation for replacement windows which she knew nothing about and the last one with a logo that she vaguely remembered but couldn't identify. She opened the letter and read the contents. For a moment she said nothing and then she passed it on to Carlotta "Would you read this dear, your eyes are better than mine and I don't quite understand it."

Carlotta studied the letter then looked at Bette quizzically "You have written books?"

"No. Well yes but ages ago and they weren't much good, I sent off a few manuscripts but no-one wanted to publish any of them."

Carlotta smiled broadly "Well this letter says these people like your book and they do want to publish it and they want to negotiate with you for the film rights."

Bette put on her glasses and held out her hand for the letter. "That can't be. It was ages ago. They must have me mixed up with someone else."   Now she recognised the publisher's logo and Carlotta was correct, they did actually want to publish the book – her book, she was stunned.

Carlotta took out her mobile, tapped in the publisher's number and thrust it toward her friend "You had better speak to them Bette, the letter is five weeks old."

Bemused and hardly able to martial her thoughts she stumbled over her words but the kindly receptionist congratulated her and assured her that Mr Harris would telephone her as soon as he returned to the office. Bette gave her own number for contact and the line was disconnected. "Charlie, I think it's time for sherries all round."

Mr Harris proved to be charming and supportive. Apparently he had taken over as CEO and wanting to improve the company image, retrieved some of the manuscripts discarded by the old guard looking for new talent, and according to him he thought her book was a winner.

Over the next few weeks the editing was completed, a suitable cover was chosen and Bette was advised to open a bank account into which royalties would be paid. The most difficult bit for Bette was giving some sort of resume of her life which Mr Harris assured her would be of interest to any reader, but as she hadn't done anything extraordinary she rather struggled with that idea.   Eventually the finished article was sent to print and several copies were proudly displayed in the lounge of The Briars where there was a general air of excitement and good will towards Bette. Matron arranged for the local newspaper to do an article on their most accomplished resident and for a special celebratory tea to mark the occasion.

Things settled down for several months during which time Bette bought herself a second hand computer. Her enthusiasm for writing had been given a boost and although her fingers were a little gnarled she managed quite well, although familiarising herself with Windows and Word took a while.

It was a beautiful Spring day. Charlie had gone off for his afternoon nap and she had settled down at her little desk when her mobile rang. "Am I speaking to Mrs Warren."

"Yes, who is this please?"

"I'm Mr Nash from the bank. I wondered if you could call in to see us over the next day or so, at your convenience of course."

Bette's heart raced, had Steven left more debts? "Oh, yes, I suppose so. Have I done something wrong?"

There was a chuckle on the end of the 'phone, "Not at all Mrs Warren. No it's just that you have rather a lot of money in what is just a current account and we would like to help you take advantage of our other products which would serve you much better. Could you possibly call in tomorrow morning, say between ten and eleven?"

Bette agreed that she could and then immediately rushed round to bang on Charlie's door, she just had to tell someone – this was unreal.

Mr Nash was pleasant and helpful. He could see that Bette was shocked at the amount of money that had accrued and suggested that she should consult a financial advisor in the near future if not now.

It had been almost a year since that meeting and she and Charlie were once again back in her little apartment supping their after lunch tea. "Penny for them Bette; you hardly said a word all through lunch.

Bette wandered over to the window and watched the daffodils swaying in the breeze. "I've paid all the debts that Steven left Charlie and now I'm not sure."

"Not sure of what?"

"What I should do now." Charlie waited for her to continue "You see I've got all this money Charlie and they want to turn my book into a film, which will mean I'll have even more money, much more than I ever dreamed of – or wanted for that matter."

"Well that's a problem most people would be more than glad of, I...."

"Well I can't stay here. It's not fair. This place is really for people without money not for the likes of me." Charlie had a feeling that he knew what she was going to say, and he didn't want to hear it. "I can afford to buy my own house now you see. I've grown to like it here you see but..."

"But it's time you moved on and said goodbye to us. Of course it is Bette and you should be proud of yourself, no-one deserves such luck more than you."

Bette turned back into the room and sat facing Charlie, "Actually Charlie, I was hoping that you would come with me. I'd really miss your company if I had to live on my own."

Charlie was nonplussed; he had known she would have to move on and had been dreading it but he had not seen this coming.

Bette stood and put a hand on his shoulder "Oh Charlie, I'm so sorry if I've upset you – I wasn't taking you for granted honestly and I'm so sorry if I've offended you, I..."

Charlie stood and gathered Bette into his arms. "Oh Bette, I thought I was going to lose the best friend I've ever had. Of course I'm not offended as long as you're sure you want me around." He stepped back, "I'll earn my keep mind, do all the jobs that need it so..."

"So I can live like 'lady muck'," she stuck out her hand smiling, "Suits me fine, shake on it."

It took a few weeks for Bette to find her ideal house in Torquay and almost three months before she actually took possession. It was of a modern design with plenty of light and stunning views overlooking the bay. It had large airy rooms so that the few pieces she and Charlie had brought with them looked lost and rather sad. Nonetheless, they were overjoyed to get their lives back and they set about making lists of things needed, not the least of which was a car.

One month later the house looked much more like a home with comfy furniture and colourful Chinese rugs setting off the beautiful tones of the oak parquet flooring. Her finishing touch had been to hang the newly framed black and white photograph of her wedding day in pride of place on the chimney breast above the inset fire – if only her darling Bob could be here. They had invited Matron, Carlotta and a few friends from The Briars along for a house warming celebration and Bette had felt very grand hiring a caterer for the occasion. She had to admit to herself that being reasonably wealthy had its' compensations.

A few days later Tom, the young reporter that she had spoken to before, rang to ask if Bette was willing to give another interview for the local newspaper in the light of her new found celebrity. She agreed and she, Charlie and Tom had a very convivial afternoon chatting about her good fortune whilst drinking tea and eating cakes.   Two days later while thumbing through a well known tabloid they were dismayed to see their faces smiling out at them under the heading Pensioner Set To Make Fortune From First Book and worse than that there was a picture of her house and a description of its' whereabouts.   Bette was bitterly disappointed; she had thought Tom such a nice young man.

Since the newspaper article she had been expecting Steven's visit so it was no surprise when within the week he arrived at her door virtually concealed behind the most enormous bouquet. He stood awkwardly in the hall facing his unsmiling mother.

He offered the bouquet as he pushed the front door to with his heel – he was in, "I hope you like these Mum. I chose pink – I know it's your favourite colour and..."

"What do you want Steven?"

"Oh Mum I've been so worried about you. You've been on my mind all this time, but Cherie had an accident and I just couldn't leave her and …."

"You've a Cambridge degree and that is all you can come up with? Where's your imagination boy! Anyway I won't ask you in as I'm sure you're busy and you mustn't leave poor Cherie on her sick bed. Oh, and while I think of it perhaps she would benefit from the flowers – I have plenty."

The Petite Chronicles

This was not going well. Steven was faced with a different mother. She used to be so malleable and eager to please but he didn't like this new version. He tried a different tack. "Actually Mum, I haven't been at all well either – I haven't been able to work for quite a while and what with us both being poorly we are a bit short," time to play the considerate loving son, "Still, not to worry about that, I'm much more interested in how you are. You seem to be getting on well," he looked around at the delicate pieces of antique furniture and noted the softness of the deep pile carpet that ran through the hall and up the stairs, "So what have you been doing with yourself?"

"It's no good Steven. I don't want you in my house, now please take your flowers and leave."

Charlie came down the stairs and at the sight of him Steven's attitude changed. "Oh, now I see it! No time for your own blood is that it? You'd rather live here with your fancy man than bother with your own son. It's disgusting! A woman of your age – what do you think Dad would say about all this? He'd ….."

Bette's voice was very level – he couldn't control her any more. "He'd ask you to leave. I don't need to explain myself to you but I will say this for Charlie's sake." She put a hand on her friend's arm "Charlie is not my fancy man but he is a wonderful man and he is my best friend. The only man I ever loved or wanted was your father and I will never forgive you for breaking his heart and sending him to an early grave. Now just go and don't come back."

Steven threw the bouquet onto the floor in a fit of pique. He wanted to shake his mother, "You won't be hearing the last of this. I'm your son and you can't just cut me off from …"

"From my money? Oh yes I can Steven, and I have. I have made a will and had it attested to that I am of sound mind and body, and you my dear heartless son will never get one penny – ever, so you had better get back to your dear wife and give her the good news."

Charlie opened the door and helped a protesting Steven over the threshold. He closed and bolted it behind the unwelcome visitor and turned to comfort Bette. She had been very strong but now felt as weak as a kitten and was unable to stop the tears that ran down her face.

"You did well Bette. I'm proud of you; that can't have been easy."

She squeezed Charlie's hand trying to smile, "I don't know about you my friend but I feel in need of a sherry."

She had faced the past and won the battle with her son although the hurt would never go away. She supposed it was a victory of sorts, but as with many victories it was bitter sweet.

Claire's Outing

The pale Winter sun bathed the garden in the early morning light and Claire clasped her coffee cup tightly between her hands as she gazed at blue tits swinging on fat-balls which hung from Phil's bird table. Her eyes filled with tears as she remembered how he would sit and watch in wonder at the variety of birds he had encouraged into their little haven soon after he had built it. He had been gone nine months now and she missed him so much. She clasped her cup harder and choked back a sob that was threatening to unleash the pent up misery of her grief.

She took a bite from her toast but she could not swallow it, her mouth was too dry, she was too nervous. Her butterflies returned and she wondered about visiting the toilet again. "Come on now girl, there's no turning back Lyn is expecting you and you've just got to damn well do it."

Claire and Phil had been happily married for forty five years when he had died suddenly of a heart attack. There had been no warning, he wasn't overweight and had always been active. The memory of that dreadful day in July would remain with her for the rest of her life. He had gone into the garden after lunch to mow the lawn but had collapsed in the garden shed. The shock had nearly killed her too and she was even now struggling to pull herself together and fill the huge dark void that had been all she could see since his death.

Phil had been the best of husbands but she realised now that since their retirement he had gradually taken over many of the things that she used to do to the point that she had lost a great deal of confidence in herself , particularly when it came to driving. Their car had sat in the garage since his death and she had not even so much as looked at it until a few days ago. Forcing herself to make the effort she had arranged to meet her friend Lyn in town for coffee and she was determined that she was going to drive herself and now, as a consequence, she was trembling with nerves. She had prepared for her outing over the last week by driving at first just to the end of a cul-de-sac around the corner and then venturing further afield each day,

The Petite Chronicles

but today would be a real test as she knew the town centre would be busy and she would have to negotiate the underground car park. The thought turned her stomach once again; perhaps she should cancel and give herself another week. "No, for goodness sake Claire, you used to drive everywhere without even thinking about it. Phil would be disappointed at you being such a fool."

She left the toast and coffee and changed her clothes with fumbling hands. She checked her bag once again, money, glasses, driving licence, and placed it on the hall table. She would be early but rather than lingering and tying herself further in knots she decided that she would leave now; she could always kill an hour by looking around the shops and she wanted to make sure that she had plenty of time to park. She checked herself once more in the mirror having to concentrate hard not to smudge her lipstick as her hands were so unsteady.

The car started first time and she pulled onto the drive stopping to watch the garage door close behind her. Heart pounding she left the safety of her home and with hands clutching the wheel firmly set out to drive the three miles into town. Gradually the tension in her body eased. It was almost as though the years had slipped away and her confidence grew with every few hundred yards. She stopped at the entrance barrier, took her ticket and drove into the bowels of the shopping centre. Good job she was early as there were loads of empty spaces. She pocketed her ticket, checked her bag for money once again and after *locking the car, walked with slightly wobbly legs to the lift.*

"Claire. I'm so glad you came. I hope you haven't been waiting long. There was quite a queue to get into the car park and I was worried that you'd think I wasn't coming."

"Hi. No, not at all; I was a bit early actually so I've been shopping." She pulled out her new purchase with a flourish. "Got myself a new handbag, what do you think?" Lyn said she loved it but she didn't really care, it wasn't as though she needed a bag, but somehow buying it had reinforced her sense of achievement, of freedom from the self imposed purdah she had been living in since Phil's death.

The two friends enjoyed their coffee and indulgent cake and Claire really laughed for the first time in months. Somehow everything seemed more colourful, and her senses to noises and smells that somewhere along the way she had lost were re-awakened. "I've got to run, I've a hair appointment this lunchtime, but shall we do the same next week, same time?"

"That would be absolutely lovely Lyn, I've really enjoyed myself today. You've done me the world of good."

"I'm so glad to hear it love. Just remember, you must take care of yourself, and from now on the only way is up."

Claire pointed her hand to the sky and smiled, "See you next week, and thanks."

Back home she was just about to tuck into a baked potato and ham salad when the 'phone rang. "Hi

Mum, just returning your call. I meant to ring you yesterday about the weekend, what time do you want me to pick you up?"

"That's why I rang dear. No need to come for me, I'll drive down. If I aim to get to you around noon will that be ok?"

There was a pause, then "But you haven't driven since...."

"I haven't done a lot of things since losing your Dad dear and it's about time I did."

"Are you sure, only...."

"I know dear but it's ridiculous you coming all the way here just to pick me up when I have a perfectly good car doing nothing. You and Gary have been wonderful to me over the last few months but now you've no need to worry. Your old Mum is back and I can't wait to see young James cut his cake. Got to go now dear as my salad is getting cold, love you." She chuckled to herself as she put the phone down.

She switched on two table lamps and the small television before drawing the curtains in the conservatory. The light was fading but she could just make out the blue tits who were still hanging on the fat-balls. Tomorrow she would buy some nuts and seeds, Phil would like that.

Excerpt from Trudie's novel

White Gold

PROLOGUE

MAY 1789

Christy Duggan hauled on his oar as he and his fellow crewmen rowed out to The Elizabeth with the last of the stores needed for their impending voyage. He looked down at his well honed muscles flexing and relaxing under his sweat moistened skin as the oar moved back and forth.   He was a sturdily built young man with a physique that many would envy and a face that,
though not strikingly handsome, was nonetheless pleasant and even featured.   He was a newcomer to the existing crew on The Elizabeth and to all intents and purposes was every inch the affable, accommodating recruit that he purported to be, his external appearance giving no clue that on the inside he was a poison filled vessel with a soul as black as Hades; a cruel and twisted being with nothing but hate in his heart.

He had tracked down Jake Faraday and his runt of a companion with just one aim, to kill them.   To make them suffer as he had done since they had slaughtered his lover Charlie. Since Charlie's death he had been haunted by the sight that had met him that dreadful day in a seedy lodging house in Calais where his lover had met his end, throat slit and kneeling in a pool of blood in a parody of prayer.   He had to admit to himself that he had been a little jealous when Charlie had refused his offer to help dispatch the runt, resenting the obsession he seemed to have for the boy. If only he had insisted on going along Charlie would still be alive and those two bastards would be dead – no doubt about it. *"Oh Charlie, if only, if only."*

He strained pulling against the white capped waves that seemed determined to push the small craft back to shore, but the grimace on his face was not from effort, his face was contorted with hatred as he looked back at the party still on the jetty saying their last farewells.

Lizzie and John Faraday hugged their son Jake and his best friend India whom they had come to love as their own; all four of them trying to quell the tears that were threatening to engulf them.   "Come on Ma, we'll be back before you know it.   It's just a straightforward trip to the islands and then on to visit George, Beau and the others to see how they've settled in Jamaica. We'll be gone less than a year and with all that's going on at Spinnaker I bet you won't even miss us."

Lizzie held her son's face in her hands. "You promise me son, you'll stay away from any trouble and," turning to India and pinching his cheek, " that you'll bring this rascal back in one piece. Promise me now or you'll not be going."

Jake picked his mother up and swung her round. "How can we possibly stay away for long?   There's no-one can cook like you Ma, and I'm missing your meat pie and dumplings already."

Lizzie blushed "Oh, you silly young 'un, I'm being serious!" Jake turned to his Pa. "I'm glad Eli is staying with you Pa. You've got so many things to see to so don't forget now, any extra help, anything you need, just get it. I've made provision for you to have all the money you may need so don't go trying to do everything yourself, not with you having been so ill and all. I'm really looking forward to seeing your new workshop being finished when I get back so you'd better get a shift on!"

John put an arm round both men - they were boys no longer, both extremely handsome but very different. Jake was tall, strong and tanned with a broad chest, long strong legs and a thick head of chestnut hair that was tied at the nape of his neck. India was almost the same height with a lighter but well muscled frame. His olive skin and short glossy black hair portraying that he did not share his ancestry with his adopted family. "Get off with you then, and Jake try to put Alice and all that has happened from your mind. None of those damned Villiers are worth a second thought, you´re ten times better than them – we all are." Seeing the pain in his son´s eyes he regretted his last words as soon as he had uttered them. He squeezed Jake hard. "Just do like your Ma says and stay out of trouble!"

Jake and Indy climbed into the last dinghy to leave the jetty, both taking an oar, unable to see their loved ones clearly through tear filled eyes.

Chapter One

Jake leant over the side watching the ship - his ship - slice through the oily navy water like a warm knife through butter. He had purchased the three-masted barque the year before from Martin Coleman, an experienced seaman who loved the ship but was struggling to afford maintenance costs. The two men had struck a deal to include all repairs and refurbishments on condition that Martin Coleman and his crew would remain with the ship for the duration of this one last voyage. Only a handful of the men had declined to join Jake but there had been no difficulty in making up numbers with volunteers from Poundsmill.

Jake was so proud; she was a beautiful ship, now slick and gleaming in her black and gold livery. He had re-named her Elizabeth after his beloved mother and had added a new figurehead carved out in her likeness.

It was a beautiful sunny day and a gentle breeze caressed the sails above gently coaxing The Elizabeth onward. They had been at sea for ten days and the weather so far had been clement; progress was steady if a little slower than generally anticipated, but time was of no real consequence on this voyage.

Jake knew he should be the happiest man on earth - he knew he was certainly one of the most fortunate - and yet he was weighed down by a sadness that he just could not shake off. He sighed deeply then turned back to his cabin nodding an acknowledgement to any of the crew that he encountered but unable to raise a smile. He sat at the chart covered table and rested his head on folded arms drowsily letting his mind wander.

So many things had happened in the seven years that had passed since that fateful day Eli had crashed, wounded and delirious, into his life setting off a chain of events that lead to him being pressed, at the age of just thirteen, into a life of misery serving as a powder monkey on the warship Huron; it seemed like a lifetime ago. It had been a dreadful time made bearable only by the friendship he had formed with his dear friend India. They had both suffered at the hands of Charlie

Croucher, a monster of a man and Jake shuddered remembering the time when he thought India was dead and he had lost his friend forever.

The Huron had been their home for many months but it had been crippled in a storm and been towed to safety by a privateer, Sir Henry Throgmorton. He pictured Harry that first time he had seen him. So handsome with blond hair spilling around his shoulders, outlandish clothes and a ready smile that had lifted Jake´s spirits from day one. He remembered how he had taken Jake under his wing opening up a whole new world to an ignorant boy, mentoring and educating him as though he were his own. He thought of the five happy years he had spent at Dragons' Lair with Harry and his men, many of whom became firm friends. He was enveloped in sadness as he remembered Harry on his deathbed, mortally wounded; Jake still felt his loss deeply.

They say that in life as one door closes another opens and in a way that was true for Jake. He had been elated to find dear India once again when fate had thrown them into the same jail but then, almost as if a price had to be paid for his happiness, he had lost Harry.

It seemed that fate had been good to India as when he had been thrown from The Huron close to death he had landed on a piece of drift wood which had carried him toward a group of islands where natives had taken him in and tended his wounds using a plant that had miraculous healing properties and which they called Kwashi. Indy had lived happily on the island for some years but his happiness was shattered when his would be bride was taken by a shark leaving India to wander wherever fate took him heartbroken and aimless, drink being his only companion.

Jake hoped they could find India's islands on this voyage and had on board in readiness a good supply of mini barrels should they have the good fortune to be allowed to harvest some of the plants with a view to propagating them back home.

The plan was then to make for Jamaica to visit John Pryor and all his old friends on their sugar plantation. He couldn't help smiling at the thought of meeting up with them again, John Pryor, Beau, George and even Boxer - he couldn't wait. After Harry's death his loyal crew had voted to move to Jamaica and start up a legal co-operative growing sugar cane. This had been Harry's dream and long term plan for himself and his men so they could at last live in peace and harmony and without danger, away from the life of piracy which had ultimately cost him his life. Harry had left Jake his share of prize money which he in turn had donated to the cause along with his own, enabling all those at Dragons Lair to follow Harry's dream to freedom. Even now, two years later, Jake still found it hard to believe that Harry, having no family and loving Jake as a son had made him his heir, leaving him the whole of the Throgmorton Estate and many riches besides. It just didn't seem real.

Longing to return home he had parted company with his pirate friends as they headed for their new life in Jamaica and had set out with India for England. On their journey home fate had once again intervened when they had encountered Charlie Croucher in Calais and Jake relived the awful day when he had been forced to kill him in order to protect India. Hounded for the murder, they had narrowly escaped capture by stealing a small dinghy, and he remembered fondly the Halfpennies who had been so kind to them when they had fetched up frozen and virtually penniless on the shores of Kent. They had eventually reached Jake's home to find his Pa injured and close to death but India's Kwashi had brought him back from the brink to make a full recovery.

Jake sighed heavily as he remembered how he had carried out Harry's last wish to deliver a gift and a message to his old love Catherine Mainwaring, now Lady Villiers, and in doing so met her daughter Alice with whom he had been immediately smitten. Their friendship had grown into love and, being now a very wealthy young man, Jake had asked Lord Villiers for Alice's hand in marriage but had been shocked and embarrassed to be turned down flat and to be shown the door.

He remembered how his cheeks had burned with shame and anger at the way he had been dismissed. He was a wealthy man true, but still a low born carpenter's son and obviously not good enough for his Lordship - well, to hell with them! He tortured himself daily with Alice's words; how could she have said she loved him and would be his wife when all the time he had been nothing but a joke, something to amuse her until she returned to society in London. Jake turned her words over and over in his mind until finally the gentle movement of the ship made him drift off to sleep.

He woke to the noise of the cabin door opening, then closing. Hearing nothing more he looked up to see India grim faced and silent. Yawning he rubbed his hands over his face "What's up Indy."

India grimaced and reached into his shirt retrieving two sheets of parchment, one with a broken seal, the other intact. "I dunno 'ow to say this Jake, but 'ere goes anyway." He took a deep breath and launched into his speech. "Just before we left Poundsmill I was give these two letters and had to promise that I wouldn't show them to yer till we was well out to sea, for yer own safety like. It's been real hard for me keeping them from you. I bin feeling bad about it but I believed what she said about you being best out of it, so that's why I kept 'em till now."

Jake looked perplexed "Who's she?" India stuck out his chin ready to defend himself for his duplicity. "They're from Lady Villiers, one to you and one to me and.."

At the mention of her name Jake slammed his fist down onto the table. "What the hell are you doing with anything of hers? Her bloody ladyship is far too good to have anything to do with the likes of us, don't you know that yet?"

"Now hold your 'orses Jake, at least give her a chance and hear what she has to say." Jake snatched the letters from India's proferred hand and slung them across the room.

"There is nothing I want to hear from that woman, or any of the Villiers family for that matter so bugger off and leave me alone." India, usually very even tempered glared at Jake, and picked up the unopened letter from the floor.

"Ok then, if you won't look at it I'll read it and," raising his voice "you can bloody well sit there till I've finished."

He ripped open the seal, his guilt at deceiving his

friend adding fuel to his anger, and began to read the contents. As he read, it became clear that Lord and Lady Villiers had not rejected Jake at all, in fact they had been prepared to welcome him into their family as their son-in-law, before that is a certain Robert Shorcross, an arrogant man to whom Jake had taken an immediate dislike, had threatened them with blackmail. His father, an eminent politician and aristocrat, had been shot dead by Harry Throgmorton in a duel and Harry had become a wanted man who would face the gallows if caught. Shorcross had found out that Catherine Mainwaring, as she then was, had been instrumental in getting Harry out of the country and he was threatening to expose her to the authorities and all society unless he was allowed to marry Alice and take over half of the Villiers estate as a dowry. They were all heartbroken at having to send Jake off but knew he would put himself in danger by challenging Shorcross had he known the truth.

The letter went on to explain that in order to fob their blackmailer off as long as possible they were taking Alice on a trip around Europe for an indefinite period in the hope that they could all find a solution to their woes by the time Jake returned.

"And she says Alice loves only you and she is so sorry to have made you so unhappy but they thought it was the only way they could get rid of yer, for yer own protection - more or less. So there yer go Jakey boy, you got them all wrong didn't yer."

Jake bemused, held out his hand "Give it to me, let me read it - are you sure?"

"Blimey Jake, I just told yer what it said but if yer don't believe me, here have it. Maybe now we can all have some peace and you can stop walkin about like Charlie Croucher's come back to haunt yer."

Jake read and re read Lady Catherine's words. It was such a nice letter and she, they, really did like him and, best of all, smiling from ear to ear, he read those precious words - Alice loved him. How could he have doubted her? How could he bear the next few months away without seeing her, touching her? He laughed out loud and swung out of his chair.

"What yer doin Jakey? You look like a bleeding madman grinning like that."

"What I'm doing my friend is getting falling down drunk. She loves me Indy." he flung his arms to the heavens. "They love me - what do you think of that!"

"Well me old turnip, I think if you're gonna get drunk I better show you 'ow to do it - I'm an expert."

As they stepped out onto the deck Jake's face clouded over. "That Shorcross bastard had his eye on Alice, I knew it! I'll take the smirk off his face when I get my hands on him, and if I have anything to do with it he won't be getting his grubby hands on any of the Villiers estate that's for sure. On the other hand he'll get much more than he bargained for from me, and that's a promise."

"Good job you're well out of it for now then ain't it! I've had enough of running from the law!"

After a couple of seconds of friendly sparring the two friends linked arms and strode along the deck engaging in friendly banter with their shipmates as they made their way to the galley, everyone noticing the sudden change in Jake. He was cock-a-hoop. His world was now perfect. Indy was jabbering on as was his wont as they made their way along the deck and Jake noticed, not for the first time, that the young man who had joined the ship at Poundsmill turned his back on them as they went past. There was something familiar about him but try as he may he could not recall where or indeed if, he had seen him before.

Christy Duggan watched the two men swan by laughing and joking. Under his breath he swore "I'll see the bastards get what they deserve Charlie, don't you worry. It won't be quick but it will be painful that I promise you.

They had been at sea for six weeks when, by Jake's reckoning, they reached the area where the Huron had been attacked. All was quiet and serene now, a far cry from the day they had been stranded crippled by storm damage with a French frigate bearing down on them. He remembered the havoc wrought by the cannon shot that had burst onto his gun deck, slaughtering several of the crew; the screams as men laying dead and dying. He could taste the smell of cordite and blood and guts - it sent a shudder to his very marrow.

He mustered his thoughts and joined India and Martin who stood around the chart table studying their maps closely. The only one who was confident that he could find India's islands was India. "I'm telling yer. The currents took me right up to them islands and I know I can get you there. I can watch the currents see and go by the stars. Old Narntac taught me all about them things and I ain't forgot 'em."

Martin looked very sceptical. He was a good man concerned for the safety of his crew and for the ship. Jake thought back to Eli telling him about his friend

Junti and how he could read the sea almost as though there were pathways that could be followed, and made a decision.

"I think we should wait until nightfall so that Indy can study the stars and see what he says then. Whatever happens, it won't do any harm to rest up for the day and we can make any decisions tomorrow when we are all fresh."

Looking at Martin India spoke "Sounds good to me, how about you?"
Not having any better solution for the moment he agreed and left the cabin to give the order to haul in the sails.

The ship was strangely quiet as they waited out the day. Some men played cards or sat around talking but most of them took to their bunks to snooze the warm afternoon away, grateful for some respite from the never ending chores.

Christy Duggan lay in his hammock gazing at his miniature of Charlie Croucher. He had been so grateful to Charlie for lifting him out of his existence of numbing poverty and showing him how to live the good life, and he had grown to love him - he had loved him more than he had ever thought it possible. His lover had introduced him to so many things, good food, expensive clothes and some things that he had not had much stomach for initially but Charlie had been right, he soon got a taste for it and as their perverted and cruel appetites grew they had relentlessly hunted down their victims with relish.

It was like Charlie said, most of the boys had such miserable lives that they were doing them a favour in the long run, they would soon be dead anyway, either from starvation or disease. He became aroused as he let his mind run free, back to those times he and Charlie had enjoyed together. Even now he remembered the thrill that had coursed through his veins at having the power of life or death over another human being, and the euphoria that came when the deed was done leaving them satiated, at least for a short time. His next victims were going to be Jake Faraday and that tar brush friend of his. Oh how he was going to enjoy himself!

Night fell and Jake and Martin stood quietly alongside India as he studied the firmament above them, both much relieved when he spoke "Yep, see that long thin trail of small stars that looks like a wisp of smoke and then the two much bigger ones to the right of it? Well we need to aim for 'em and then keep 'em on the starboard side. I'm sure now we're that close I'll be able to read the waters once the sun is up but," pointing due south "that's definitely where we need to head for."

Jake marked their position on the ship's map then charted a course due south; he had enough confidence in his friend to ask Martin to hoist sail and continue on their journey through the balmy moonlit night.

Once the sun was up India seemed to be able to steer instinctively toward their goal. He had been standing in the bow of the ship since daybreak concentrating hard, studying the waters when he suddenly cried out "Gawd almighty! Look, look, the sea children, they've come to meet us."

Jake headed for the bow wondering what all the commotion was about and saw his friend jumping up and down, waving and pointing and calling out to anyone within hearing. Following India's directions he looked over the side and saw a group of huge fish speeding alongside the ship, leaping out of the water as though spring loaded and he could just make out India screeching something about children.

His friend's excitement was infectious and remembering India's tale of the creatures that had pushed him ashore he laughed out loud. We've made it lads, we've made it!"

Sure enough, as dusk was falling, they heard a cry from the crow's nest, "Land - Ho." Hauling all sails bar the foresails to slow their speed they maintained their course, anchoring just off a small group of islands until sun up.

At Jake's request the whole crew were assembled on deck so that he could run over once again the reason for visiting the islands, and so that India could acquaint them with some of the local customs.

"You all know we have come in the hope of being able to harvest a pretty remarkable plant which has proven to be a wonderful medicine. Once, if, we get permission to lift some of these plants I am hoping that they can be transplanted and grown successfully, some in the sugar plantation we are going on to in Jamaica, and some once we get back to England. All I can is say that when used properly, this plant works miracles. I appreciate that many of you are sceptical about my claims, but there is no doubt that it saved my father's life and God willing, if we are successful, it will save many other poor souls. Now, over to India."

Most of the men were already acquainted with these customs as India had spent many hours amusing his shipmates with tales from his past and with life on the islands. Many were indeed sceptical about the benefits of some plant but as they were being well paid to ply their trade they were happy to humour their delusional friends.

India was trembling with emotion. He never truly thought he would return to this place and the thought of seeing Narntac and his family, the family that had once been his, filled him at once with wild elation, dread and overwhelming sadness. He felt the physical pain of losing Narnsee strike him once again and was so grateful to have Jake alongside him to share this journey.

"Jake's right. The people on these islands used their medicine on me or I'd 'av been a gonna and that's for sure. They was real good to me and I lived here with 'em for years, but I need to tell yer a few things. For starters, they don't wear many clothes, and the wimmin don't have no tops on."

This gave rise to a few ribald jokes and laughter.

"It ain't funny! That's the way they are; they just don't need 'em and they don't see no wrong in it. They ain't got none of our bad habits either. They don't steal, don't know what lies are and they don't do no-one any wrong, so we gotta be the same - or else!"

Martin Coleman took up India's warning. "You heard what India said. These people are very different from us so while we are here we respect them and their customs, and be assured gentlemen, that anyone who steps out of line will be locked in the brig for the duration of the voyage! That is all. Now let's get those dinghies into the water. The order was given but before the first craft had hit the surface several canoes appeared from inside the island's protective reef making their way speedily to The Elizabeth.

Harbour Lights

Matron waved at Julia as she entered St Mary's Hospice, "Hello dear, how are you today?"

"I'm fine thanks, how's Mum?"

"She's having a good day dear – seems in very good spirits. She was having a little nap when I looked in earlier but I know she'll be happy to see you."

Julia smiled and pushed open the fire door that led to Mum's corridor. The familiar smell of Lily of the Valley filled the air, a smell that she would never forget. She couldn't help thinking that it was a beautiful place and much as she loved her Mum, she was glad that she would end her days here. Matron bustled up to join her putting a hand on her arm, "You know it won't be long now dear don't you. These are precious times." Julia swallowed hard and nodded as Matron opened the door.

Sandra was supremely happy. Geoff had just been demobbed and now he was home for good. There would be no more weeks of worry and longing and now they could plan their future together. They sashayed around the dance floor to the dulcet tones of the Platters singing 'their song' pressing close consumed with desire fuelled by their nearness to each other, "Oh Sandy I can't wait till we are married. I love you so much it hurts."

She leant back into his arms and looked into his handsome face dappled now by shadows from the glitter ball above. "I love you too Geoff, and I'll love you forever and ever."

Geoff sighed, warm breath caressing her ear "Oh Sandy."

The Petite Chronicles

"Sandy, Mrs Carter, there's someone here to see you dear." Sandra slowly opened her eyes as the dream faded and the ever efficient Matron plumped up her pillows. "There we are dear, that's much more comfy isn't it," and without waiting for a reply she sped off.

"Oh, hello dear, I was just with your Dad – he was so handsome you know, so very handsome." She sighed deeply, "He's waiting for me." She squeezed her daughter's hand "Do you know I love him just as much today as I did the day we married." She stared off dreamily then snapped back into the present, "And how are you today?"

"I'm fine Mum but more to the point, how are you?"

"No, I want to hear all about you and the boys, and how is that man of yours treating you?"

When Julia had brought Richard home some thirty years ago Sandra had not been able to hide her disappointment. Her dearest Geoff had died in an accident when Julia was only four years old and she had vowed to herself that she would not let him down and their daughter would be given all the opportunities that they had missed out on. She'd hoped to acquire a son-in-law with gravitas, a doctor say, or an architect but instead Julia seemed besotted with an apprenticed engineer.

For quite some years she and Richard had been at loggerheads, with him being unable to do anything right in her eyes. She had mellowed slightly when the twins were born and had been touched when they christened one of the boys Geoffrey, but she still felt that her dear Julia had married beneath herself. Over the years however she had come to admit that her daughter's happiness should be paramount and there was no doubt that Richard succeeded in that department, and it seemed he had become very successful in his chosen career.

Money seemed to be no object with family holidays by the seaside every year (invitations to which she consistently refused), and then as the boys grew holidays abroad in the summer and skiing in the spring.   It wasn't until she was first diagnosed that she really took stock and had to admit to herself that Julia had actually picked absolutely the right man for her.   She had wasted all those years sulking because things didn't go to plan and had been blinded by her own obstinacy and the bitterness she felt at losing her beloved Geoff.   Unfortunately, there was no turning back the clock but she resolved to change in the time she had left and embrace life with the family to the full.

As Julia visited every day there was no real news but they would reminisce a little then listen to the Platters on the little player that she had taken in so that Mum could listen to 'their tune' the words of which, according to Matron, were now known by all the staff as it was played so often.

"I'll be off now Mum. Is there anything you want me to bring in, are you ok for ..."

Sandy waved her question away with a smile and snuggled down into her pillows. "You just look after that man of yours; he's a good 'un you know." She pointed to the player, "I'd like to be with your Dad now, can you're?"

"Love you Mum." Julia bent over, kissed her mother and switched on the player. She turned to wave goodbye but

Mum's eyes were closed and she was off somewhere with her love.   She left the room to the strains of Harbour Lights, tears clouding her eyes.

Josh's Dilemma

Sergeant Josh McGiven sat at his desk regretting the late night work and the one too many whiskies he'd downed in an effort to get a decent nights ' sleep. Life hadn't been going too well over the last year, what with Carol hounding him for more child allowance and being overlooked for the promotion that he thought was in the bag, and now he was being pressured to find the perpetrator of a series of seemingly aimless murders which had them all baffled and which was putting his unit under rather unfavourable scrutiny. No one had said anything thus far but Josh and his team were well aware that their failing efforts were being closely monitored.

He took the files that he'd left on his desk the night before and spread them out. He picked up the file of the first victim and decided to start at the beginning and re-interview their one and only witness. He saw that she was a Mrs Whitlock and he noticed that she lived just two streets away from his rented flat. He pondered on the details – an elderly woman who had found the victim after deciding to investigate two loud bangs that she had heard nearby. As she'd approached the victim she had seen someone running away but her eyes were not good enough to make out any details, other than she assumed it to be a man and he seemed to move rapidly. When asked she thought his clothing to be dark coloured.

Josh made his way to his car with the file under his arm which also contained pictures of the subsequent five victims – you never knew. Mrs Whitlock lived in a quiet leafy road on the outskirts of town in just the kind of house he and Carol always said they wanted to end up in – but that was a life time ago. He rang the bell which gave rise to a dog barking somewhere at the back of the house, and after a few minutes the door opened a few inches and the face of a very diminutive elderly lady peered out.

"Good morning madam. I'm Detective Sergeant McGiven and I wondered if I could just take a minute of your time."

Ada's heart began to thump and she hoped the young man didn't hear the quake in her voice as she asked for identity. He seemed more than happy to oblige and actually congratulated her on being so careful. She opened the door to admit him and called out to Bobby to be quiet.

Josh was shown into what Mrs Whitlock liked to call the lounge and explained that as they were not making any headway in these killings he had decided to review every case once more in the hope that something might turn up. He accepted the offer of tea glad of the opportunity to exercise his policeman's curiosity and have a look round. He noticed a photograph of a middle aged couple both dressed in army uniform that took pride of place on the mantelpiece. So, Mrs Whitlock was ex army – who would have thought.

Ada busied herself making tea. She told herself to breathe deeply as her mind raced. What did this man want? What did he know? She put the teapot, cups and saucers and plate of biscuits on a tray and, trying to sound as jolly as she could she spoke to Bobby, "Come on Bobby we've got a visitor – come in and meet the nice man."

Josh thought Ada, as she insisted upon being called, to be absolutely charming, and her little dog Bobby was just the kind of companion he would like. Never mind, back to business. He opened the file and read out Ada's statement asking her to think hard, could she remember anything else at all that she had left out. Ada sat, pretending to concentrate, "Well, only that I knew they were gun shots. I'm ex army you see so I knew the sound. Not that I used firearms of course, Stan – that's my husband – we were in admin – logistics and that sort of thing." Ada looked wistful, "I do miss him so – that's why I got Bobby, so I wouldn't be on my own".

Josh was reluctant to submit Ada to any more upset but he had a job to do so he asked her to study the faces of all the victims – it was a long shot but she might possibly know one or more of them. Ada didn't have to feign being upset – the last thing she ever wanted to do was see again the faces of the men she had killed, she took out her hankie and blew her nose. "Oh, those poor men, and so many of them but I'm afraid no, I've never seen any of them before – who were they; were they gangsters?"

Josh had to smile at the old fashioned terminology "I can't say too much Mrs Whitlock, but thank you for your time anyway, and for the refreshments."

Ada waved to her visitor as he pulled away from her house then went inside to pour a large glass of port. "Oh Bobby, that was a frightener and no mistake."

When Josh returned to the office there was a note confirming that the gun used to kill victim number six was the same as that used on all other five.

Over the next few days Josh re-interviewed the families of the first five victims, and with the passing of time and less fear of incriminating themselves, some of them spoke more freely, admitting that not all the deaths had exactly been bad news. Slowly but surely Josh was able to establish that these men had been guilty of extreme domestic violence, and having seen the partner of victim number six he had no doubts that he fell into the same category. So there was a connection and maybe a motive but what linked these families to the killer. He doubted that any of them would have the money or the nous to take out a contract – or was it one of them? He would just have to keep on digging.

It was a couple of weeks before he got around once again to visiting Julie Forbes. In truth he had been putting off visiting Shedwell. It was a miserable place and he was always worried about the condition his car would be in if it was left for more than ten minutes. He noticed how much better she was looking than the first time he'd interviewed her. The flat was clean and tidy and she had definitely put on a bit of weight which suited her – she was actually a very pretty girl. As he had done with all the others he laid out the photos of all of the victims but once more he drew a blank, Julie did not recognise anyone.

He pulled out of the estate thankful that his car was still intact, slowing down to allow an elderly woman and her pooch cross the road. Mrs Whitlock was buttoned up against the chill wind but it was Bobby that he recognised. He lowered his window, Mrs Whitlock, "What a surprise, I wouldn't have expected to see you in this area."

Ada looked up recognising him immediately and waved, but he was sure he saw a glimpse of annoyance – or was it fear in the split second before she had composed herself. "Oh Bobby and I have just been for our afternoon walk." She pointed toward the open land beyond, "We just come here occasionally – it makes a change and Bobby loves to play with other dogs." She smiled "I suppose I could say the same about you – I don't think policemen are particularly popular around here do you?"

"Just following up on a lead; do you know anyone in Shedwell?"

"Not that I'm aware of. I think some of the dog walkers may live here or here about, but we never do more than just pass the time of day."

"Can I give you a lift?"

"That is very kind of you Sergeant but my car is parked just down the road so we are fine," she looked down at her dog, "Aren't we Bobby."

Josh wished her well and continued on his way. Something had ignited his interest. It was a coincidence seeing Ada here today, and he never did like coincidences. As he drove along he told himself not to be so stupid. The case was getting to him and he was clutching at straws. By the time he reached his office he had managed to convince himself that he must be losing the plot.

He sat at his desk frowning. There was something floating around in his brain but it just wouldn't come to the fore. His hand hovered over the files that were still spread on his desk and he picked up file number two. He leafed through the pages almost trying to divine a clue and then he saw it. The words jumped out at him, the bullets were from a handgun, maybe a Beretta, and someone had scrawled in the margin *ex military*? He remembered the photograph on Ada's mantelpiece – another coincidence.

The Petite Chronicles

On a whim he decided to check up on something and within half an hour he was back knocking on the door of Julie Forbes. After assuring her that she was not in any trouble he asked her to go over her movements from a week or so prior to the murder of her partner. Julie gradually relaxed and began to describe her pretty humdrum existence which was regularly interspersed with beatings that she was thankful she no longer had to suffer. Josh asked if anything out of the ordinary had happened – anything no matter how small and seemingly insignificant.

"Well there was one time." Josh sat up, all ears.

"It was when Gary was really laying in to me. We'd well – you know, just been to bed and I was getting dressed when he started accusing me of having other men in here when he wasn't around. It was stupid of course, but he'd worked himself up into a real temper. He punched me a few times and I was really scared so I just grabbed my coat and ran outside. I didn't think what I was doing and I just ran," she hesitated.

"Go on Julie, nothing you say will get you into any kind of trouble."

"Well I just ran and because my eye had swollen, and I suppose I was crying, I just bumped into this lady – nearly knocked her over."

Josh could feel the hairs on his neck bristling.

"She was a lovely old girl. Made me get into her car and covered me up with her dog's blanket. She was really kind."

"Then what happened?"

"I saw Gary coming after me so I scooted. Didn't want to get her into trouble – he could be really nasty, and he didn't care who to. We went back indoors and of course he was lovely then, promised he wouldn't touch me ever again," she shrugged, "Some hopes."

Josh was just about to speak when Julie carried on.

"Wasn't long before he stamped on my hand and split my lip because little Eddie was crying. I don't mind telling you I was at the end of my tether by then. Anyway, I saw the old girl again when I was out shopping. I could tell she felt sorry for me. She wanted to buy me a drink and have a chat, and she was so kind and understanding that I was on the verge of asking her for help, but I saw Gary outside in the car park drumming his fingers on the steering wheel and I lost my nerve." She looked at Josh defiantly, "It's good to know there are some nice people in the world anyway."

"You say this lady had a dog; I don't suppose you know her name."

"No, but she was lovely and so was her little dog, Bobby his name was."

....

Josh's head was spinning as he drove toward Ada's house. All roads lead to Ada, but that was crazy. He was sure now that she was involved somehow, but how? Did she have an accomplice? Was she paying someone to kill these men, and if so why? Admittedly the world was a better place without them – in his opinion at least, but how were all these deaths connected? Were they being eliminated because of what they were?

Once more he heard Bobby barking when he rang the doorbell and once more Ada opened the door just a few inches and this time Josh noticed that she had put on the safety chain. "Oh, Mr McGiven, how nice to see you again." She took off the chain and let him in, "You can't be too careful with all these murders going on. Do come in and I'll make some tea and I've some freshly baked scones; now how can I help?"

The house smelled deliciously of baking and Josh was shown into the lounge. He'd brought along the same photos of the deceased men as before, but this time he'd added a few lines of description to them as he'd noticed previously that she didn't seem to bother with glasses which didn't quite tally with the poor eyesight alluded to in her witness statement.

He watched Ada carry the tray laden with tea, scones, butter and jam and realised that he'd made the common mistake of underestimating her just because she was elderly.   Yes, she had white hair and was in her seventies, but her movements were swift and agile, almost athletic.   Her mind was sharp and clear and now that he thought about it, her years in the army were evident in that everything about her home and herself was orderly and ship shape.

He spread the pictures out for her to peruse which she did, picking up each one and reading aloud the text that he had introduced – without the aid of spectacles. "Your eyesight is better than mine Ada, I couldn't do that without having my lenses in – or do you have lenses too."

He saw it then. She didn't alter her expression but he knew she was on to him. "Not for reading no, but I'm not so hot at distances." They both knew her answer was a little lame.

"These scones are delicious Ada. You'll have to give me the recipe – I live on my own now and I must be the world's worst cook." He quickly changed tack, "Do you own a gun at all? I mean, I know it isn't legal but I just wondered, with you and your husband being in the military." His words hung in the air.

Ada finished the mouth full of scone and smiled with her mouth only, "Why on earth would I have a gun and how would I get one? We were both in the military, but it's strictly forbidden to ….."

"Yes of course," he shook his head, "It was a silly thing to say."

This was surreal. Here he was eating home-made buttered scones and drinking tea with a would-be serial murderer. He took a sip from his cup – how to approach this.

The nice Sergeant was obviously preoccupied and Ada sensed the game was up. "Tell me Sergeant, if you caught this killer I suppose they would face a life in jail and...."

"For murdering six men – I should certainly think so. Whoever is guilty would spend the rest of their life locked up with absolutely no chance of release."

"Do you think you will ever catch him?"

Josh chose his words carefully "Well, we have a lot of leads that don't quite tie up, but we are piecing the jigsaw together and of course he, or she, will make a mistake eventually, they always do."

"So reading between the lines, you seem to be saying that if there were no more occurrences these murders will remain unsolved."

"That's about it in a nutshell."

"You already know the truth don't you Sergeant?" Josh choked and began to cough. He had not expected this. "Oh, it's alright. I would never harm you. It was just all those poor women you see," she dug her nails into the palms of her hands, "Those dreadful cruel men just did as they pleased and no-one was there to help – I felt it was my duty, do you see? There, I've admitted it to you but of course I'll deny ever having done so." Ada picked up the tray and spoke matter of fact, "Just thought it would be good to clear the air

Sergeant McGiven.   Now, I'll make a fresh pot of tea, and would you like another scone?

Josh was too shocked to formulate any words, so just shook his head to the affirmative.

Josh, still a little dazed climbed into his car carrying the file of photos and a recipe for Ada's fruit scones. What the hell was he going to do? He'd just spent an hour with a most unlikely murderer and he had no proof other than her admission. There were no witnesses, no gun, nothing to tie her directly to all six crimes, and the worst thing was that he had grown quite fond of the old girl.   By the time he reached his office, and after a great deal of soul searching, he had decided to keep her secret and just back peddle with his investigations, after all, doing much else would just be a complete waste of police time and public money.

Ada rinsed out the teapot and washed up the tea plates and butter knife. "Well Bobby, it's in the lap of the Gods now. First thing tomorrow we'll take a little trip out to get rid of the gun and then we'll just have to wait and see what the good Sergeant does." She bent to ruffle the dog's head, "Right my lad, we'd better get you out for your walk before the light fails."

As they strolled along to the local park Ada was deep in thought. "Well Bobby, you know I like to have a project on the go, but we can't carry on with my old one now we've been found out, so I think I'll concentrate on finding Sergeant McGiven a partner; the poor man must be lonely," she thought for a moment then reached a decision, "That Julie was a nice girl – maybe they would both like to come round for lunch one day. Yes, I think that would be a good place to start."

Bobby didn't quite understand what his mistress was saying, but he sensed her good mood and they were going to the park, so as far as he was concerned all was well in the world.

Man's Best Friend

Christopher Harmer tugged on the huge dog's lead, but the dog was going nowhere. The kennel owner came to his rescue and with a little persuasion and the bribe of a dried pig's ear Nikademus was eventually loaded into the waiting Land Rover. "Take it easy with him er.."

"Jude, just call me Jude."

Christopher had been orphaned at the age of six when his parents had been killed as their coach had plunged into a ravine in Spain. He had been staying with his Grandparents at the time and fortunately they were able to continue giving him the love and security that every well balanced child needs. Unfortunately, maybe brought on by the loss of her only son Grandma succumbed to dementia and his world was turned upside when Grandpa died suddenly leaving no-one to care for him. His only other living relative, a maiden aunt, had settled somewhere in South Africa but little was known of her whereabouts.

He had been taken into care at the age of nine and passed from one foster home to another, each stay shorter than the one before as his behaviour deteriorated. Eventually he left the chaos that was the care system and lived contentedly if not happily in a bed sit working in the offices of a well know supermarket where he liked to be known as Jude – he thought it sounded cool. He much preferred that to Christopher – that name belonged to a long abandoned little boy who he wanted to forget.

He avoided close contacts of any sort having learnt that buttoning down emotions was the only way to protect oneself from hurt. He never looked to the future, had no desire to explore the big wide world; just lived from day to day keeping everything and everyone at a distance.

Then, out of the blue, he had learnt that his aunt, who unbeknown to him had by now moved to the Scottish Highlands, had died some months before and, as he was her only living relative, she had left her entire estate to him with just one proviso. He had to take care of Nikademus, her three year old Mastif. So here he was driving to her large draughty house in her large powerful car with a decidedly unwanted large dog.

When they reached the house the dog immediately ran to his mistresses' room whimpering. "No good you looking in there you dope. She's gone and left you, just like everyone does." He threw down a bowl of food "You can eat that or not, I couldn't care less."

Man and dog reached any uneasy truce over the next few weeks and when Jude took himself off for a walk Nikademus followed behind, just as he had always done with his beloved mistress. It had been raining heavily for the past two weeks but today was dry although the sky was dark overhead and there was a cold wind blowing. He loved this weather; it suited his mood, dark and cold. As usual the dog tagged along and he began to wonder how long he would have to put up with him before he could give him away without jeopardizing his inheritance.

The stream that ran nearby was very lively, far more like a river now as it crashed over the rocks throwing spray that was blown away in an instant. He walked into the water fascinated as it raced to the top of his wellingtons drenching his socks. It was freezing. He turned back to the bank but slipped, this was not funny; he was drenched. While he was scrabbling to regain a foothold his legs were taken from under him by a broken branch which pushed him further and further downstream, and the water here was quite a bit deeper; he was scared now. He tried to stay on his feet but the force of the water kept knocking him down. It was so cold and he was getting weaker. He was fully immersed now and there seemed to be some contra current pulling him down. Struggling to keep his head above water he was vaguely aware of Nikademus barking and running along the bank, but he went under again. It was so cold but he couldn't fight any more – no strength – too cold.   He hadn't expected to die today.   What a surprise – he never thought it would end like this.

Suddenly he felt an excruciating pain which jolted him back to consciousness.   He opened his eyes to see his arm lodged in the great dog's mouth.   His saviour lay astride a fallen tree which was half in the water and he was holding onto his master for dear life.   Realising what the dog had done Jude felt an enormous rush of gratitude towards him, and was relieved beyond measure to be out of danger. With his free hand he grabbed hold of a broken branch and seeing this, the dog let go freeing him to haul himself toward the log using both arms.   He moved along the tree grabbing hold of jutting branches until eventually he managed to draw himself out of the water and stagger onto the bank before collapsing exhausted.

After a few minutes he sat up and saw Nikademus looking his way seemingly entreating him for help but then he turned his great head away and lay it back onto the log as if realising that none was coming. That was when Jude saw blood running from beneath the dog and mingling with the still frothing water.

For the first time in his adult life Jude felt emotion.   This clever dog had saved his life and the thought of him now being in distress was almost more than he could bear. With renewed adrenalin fuelled strength he worked his way along the log until he reached the dog. "Don't worry boy. I've got you. You're going to be fine." He would never know how he did it but he hoisted Nikademus out of danger and tramped across the fields to home, laying him gently on the back seat of his car and thanking heaven that the keys were still in it. It took half an hour to get to the vet and all the while he was talking to the dog who lay deathly still with his eyes closed. "You'll be alright boy. Just hang on now. We'll get you sorted in no time – don't you dare die on me now!"

Covered in blood and still ringing wet a wild man ran into Stace's veterinary practice shouting for someone to help his dog. All hands jumped to and in no time Nikademus was stretchered into theatre as Jude was handed a cup of strong coffee and quizzed as to how the pair of them had got into such a state.

Once his arm had been examined Jude was persuaded to drive to the local clinic where his wound was dressed and he was pumped full of antibiotics, and as he began once again to explain how he had come by the bite, without warning, he began to cry. Years of pent up emotion poured from him like water through a sieve. All the grief and resentment he had kept inside bubbled over and into his consciousness just as the water in the stream had bubbled into his wellingtons, and the tears just would not stop. The doctor on call decided to sedate him and keep him in overnight; it was obvious that he was in no fit state to make his own way home.

When Jude visited Nikademus the next day his heart leapt to see him alive and well, and the joy he felt at the wagging tail that acknowledged his presence was almost overwhelming.   Apparently the poor fellow had been unable to move from the fallen tree as he had dislocated his shoulder, probably in the effort of holding Jude against the pressure of the water, and he had also sustained a nasty tear across his abdomen which was now sutured and dressed.   The dog, like Jude would need a course of antibiotics but all being well would be able to go home with his master tomorrow.

Jude leant against the desk admiring the pretty receptionist and wondering if she had a boyfriend. She smiled at him "Now sir, if I could just take a few details starting with your name."

"It's Christopher, Christopher Harmer and my dog's name is Nikademus."

Meg

It was no good; Meg just couldn't sleep. The air conditioning was humming quietly and successfully keeping the moist tropical heat at bay, but it wasn't the heat that was the reason for her restlessness.

Just a few days ago her dear Ben had surprised her by proposing and presenting her with a most beautiful ring, and just to make things perfect he had whisked her away for a week to this beautiful five star hotel, but things were not perfect.

She crept stealthily from the bedroom and threw on a flimsy dress before stepping out into the sultry night. A gate at the rear of the hotel lead directly onto a private beach which was now deserted and the only sound she could hear was that of the ocean lapping gently onto the sand. She walked along the waters' edge grateful for the caress of the cooling water on her feet.

She thought of Harry and felt the inevitable trickle of tears that always accompanied the constant ache that she felt without him. She'd adored Harry almost from the first time she had laid eyes on him, and the two years they had enjoyed together before he was killed were the happiest she had ever known, but giving your heart to a serving soldier was a very risky business and she had learnt that in the very hardest way.

Three years after losing Harry she had been introduced to Ben by a mutual friend and they had immediately recognised in each other a kindred spirit and almost inevitably had grown closer and now, just one year later here she was alone wrestling with her conscience.

Just a few weeks ago her mother, who probably understood Meg better than she did herself, had asked what was wrong, and without too much prompting Meg had admitted that Harry was still in her heart, and although she loved Ben it was not in the overwhelming way that made her want to spend the rest of her life with him. Her mother had held her just as she had when a child and said she knew that Meg would do the right thing by Ben; if she really could not love him in the right way it was only fair to be honest and let him get on with the rest of his life.

Meg turned back toward the hotel entrance watching the reflection of the lamp lights ripple on the dark smooth water and disappear into nothingness. She crept back into their room and stood watching Ben sleep. He was so handsome and kind, she was going to hurt him so. She slipped off her ring and placed it on his bedside table turning away with tear filled eyes. She would spend the night on the terrace lounger. She just couldn't join him in bed now that she had made up her mind, it would be disloyal; he deserved better than that.

The slight breeze tousled her hair as she sat underneath a crescent moon wondering how on earth she could let Ben down lightly. She had been unfair to him letting things get this far and in her own way she loved him dearly and would do almost anything to avoid hurting him, but she had to do this for both their sakes.

The Petite Chronicles

She woke with Ben standing over her, ring in hand. He helped her to her feet and they clung together. Eventually Meg found her voice, "I'm sorry Ben but it's just that..."

Ben placed a finger on her lips and shook his head "I understand Meg. I know – I suppose I've always known."

My Darling Charlie

Eddie broke one of the glass panels in the dilapidated back door and both boys stood quietly, listening for any signs that they had been heard. All remained quiet so, being careful to avoid the spiteful shards Eddie slid in his arm and turned the key that was still in the lock inside holding the rickety door firm; it stuck a little but after a good push the boys were inside. The house was a few doors down from their own homes and one of a row of terraced houses in Balham that had certainly seen better days. The owner of the two up, two down had been taken off in an ambulance several days ago, presenting a golden opportunity for the friends to break in.

Looking round the very basic kitchen which was dark and dingy and smelt of mould Kenny wrinkled his nose. "Christ Eddie, there ain´t gonna be much worth nickin in here, and it stinks! When did you say the old man´s gonna be back?"

"He´s supposed to be back tomorrow so let´s get on with it. You look round down here and I´ll go upstairs." Kenny nodded and reluctantly started opening cupboard doors moaning all the time that the place was filthy and they were wasting their time as all they were going to find were cockroaches and fleas.

Eddie climbed the narrow staircase and took a cursory look around the first bedroom he came to. To say it was sparse was something of an understatement. There was just one single bed and mattress and one wooden chair. There was a grimy sink on the wall but when he turned the tap no water came out, he supposed it could be turned off at the mains but this sink had seen no action for quite some time.

The second bedroom, which fronted the street, showed more promise with its double bed and a bedside unit on either side. There was a small upholstered chair under the window but the thing of most interest was a tall chest of drawers upon which were several photographs. He squinted at the black and white photos in the gloomy room. One was of a soldier very much like the one his Gran used to have when she was alive, the other showed the same man with a woman dressed in white, obviously a wedding photo, and the other was of a small boy sitting on a stool in front of a piano.

Starting at the bottom Eddie went through the drawers but there was absolutely nothing of value, just old men´s clothes that smelt of mothballs. He reached the two smaller top drawers and this time found things of interest. There was a small box containing several medals and, at last, something that he could sell down the market, a gold pocket watch! He put the watch in his pocket and opened the adjacent draw. Inside there was a bundle of letters tied with a faded ribbon. Curiosity got the better of him; he untied the ribbon, opened a letter, and sitting on the candlewick bedspread, he began to read.

"My Darling Charlie,

I hope this letter finds you well and that you are keeping safe. Little Johnny and I are in the best of health and I´ve turned our little garden into a kind of vegetable patch so that we don´t go too hungry what with the rationing and all.

I listen to the news on the wireless every night and it´s sometimes more than I can bear when I hear what is happening over there in France. Every night I pray for your safety and so fear the knock on the door that may deliver that dreaded telegram. Just promise me that you will come home safe, that´s all I ask. Nothing in the world means more to me than you.

Loving you always, Jeannie

Eddie picked out another letter at random –

My Darling Charlie,

As I haven´t had any news of you I am hoping, no praying, that you are safe.   It´s getting a bit difficult over here, what with all the bombs dropping on the East End.   The siren goes most nights and it´s off to the shelter we go. I hope you won´t object but I´m thinking of sending Johnny away with the next lot of kids to be evacuated. We lost a couple of houses down the end of the road and the McCarthy family all went, didn´t have a chance.

It´s awful not knowing where you are or what you are doing, but keep us in your heart my darling as we keep you in ours.

Loving you always, Jeannie

Eddie had heard about kids bring evacuated but never really given it any thought. It must have been pretty frightening, and fancy having to get up every night and leg it to some shelter. He reached further down the pile.

My Darling Charlie

No news is good news so they say, so I´m praying that is so in your case. We are still getting nightly visits from the Hun but it´s not too bad as now that Johnny isn´t here I just go to the shelter like loads of others and stay there the night. I´ve started working in a kitchen that's been set up for the firemen and rescue workers. They are working so hard Charlie and some of the things they have to deal with are beyond words.

Anyhow, that's enough of me! I had a real nice letter from the headmistress of the little school that Johnny is going to and guess what? She reckons our boy is so clever that when all this bloody business is over she is going to make sure that he is put forward for a scholarship. She said that such a gifted child simply must get a good education and she is going to pull as many strings as she can to make sure that he does. Just fancy, our Johnny clever enough for a scholarship! I wonder what he will be when he grows up. Whatever it is, if he gets a good job he won't have to be content with crumbs from a rich man's table like us. He might even be a Doctor or a Solicitor, just think of that!

I must go now my love as I'm needed to help out at the kitchen. We had a really heavy raid last night so the lads will be glad of us.

Loving you always, your Jeannie

He decided he would read one more letter and then they had better scarper.

My Darling Charlie

I nearly collapsed when those soldiers knocked on the door. They had to help me indoors I was upset fearing the worst, but thank goodness all they had was good news. I know it´s not too good for you my love, losing an eye must be awful, but you are safe and you are alive, and that´s all I care about. I am so sorry that your friend Ivan didn´t make it, I know you´d grown to love him like a brother and you must be heartbroken, and believe me my heart goes out to his family as I know how I felt when I got the knock on the door.

You´ll soon be home my darling and from the sounds of it the game is up for the Hun over there in Germany, so then God willing everyone can have their loved ones back. If you write to Ivan´s family please tell them how sorry I am. I know I didn´t meet him but I feel I got to know him through your letters.

Come home to me soon my darling.

Loving you always, your Jeannie

Eddie stacked the letters back into a pile and tied them with the faded ribbon. He placed them back in the drawer then took out the pocket watch that he had intended to steal and put it back where he had found it.

He suddenly felt uncomfortable. He had encroached on someone else´s life. The old man they used to jeer at when he shuffled down to the corner shop in his slippers had become a real person to him. He had been young and virile, had a wife and child; he was a real person and had lived through horrors that Eddie knew were beyond his understanding. He wondered what had happened to his wife and little Johnny; were they dead? Did they abandon him? He looked around the dingy room shaking his head slightly; the old man had lived a full and long life and all he had to show for it was this dump.

Kenny stomped noisily up the stairs. "There´s bugger all down there except this." He held up a leather and brass telescope, "We should get a couple of quid for it down the old market."

"Put it back, and make sure you put everything back the way it was. We´re going – now."

Kenny was momentarily speechless, "What you on about, this is the only bloody thing worth having."

Eddie stood and snatched the telescope from his friend´s hand. "It´s going back and we are leaving. No arguing right!"

Kenny who had always been subservient to his friend did not argue, but turned on his heel and stomped out of the house trying, but unable to slam shut the stubbornly sticking back door.

Eddie´s Mum Marje looked up from rolling pastry. "You alright son? I didn´t hear you come in. Have you fallen out with Kenny again?"

Eddie shrugged, "Sort of."

"Bloody good job I say, he's a dead beat and you could do much better for yourself than knocking around with the likes of him. And while I'm on the subject me and your Dad won't have any nonsense this term. You are going back to school next week and if we hear of you playing truant we are going to report you to the social. We've had enough Eddie – enough!"

"OK. I've been thinking. I need to get a proper job, you know, one that pays good money so I don't have to be content with living on crumbs from a rich man's table."

Marje stopped her rolling. She had been expecting the usual row but Eddie had taken the wind completely from her sails. "That's right son. You couldn't have put it better. Me and your Dad have been tearing our hair out watching a clever boy like you throwing away chance after chance when you've got the brains to really go places and make something of yourself."

"I know Mum, I'm on it."

As he walked out from the kitchen Eddie picked up a piece of the sliced apple intended for the pie. He turned in the doorway "Any chance of making a little one for the old boy down the road? He's supposed to be coming home from hospital tomorrow and I don't suppose he'll have much in."

New Beginnings

She popped her electric toothbrush back into its' holder; one now where there used to be two. She sat on the edge of the bath overcome with sadness, reflecting that it was almost a year since Keith had left. She was better now, stronger, but in those early dark days she had been unable to see anything but a huge black hole where her life had once been.

Her instincts had told her that something was amiss even before his indifference really began to show. He wasn't interested in going on holiday, didn't want to join in any family events and was less than interested when their first grandchild had arrived. She'd pleaded with him to talk to her, to try to explain what she was doing wrong but all she ever got was the stock answer of "It's not you it's me."

She should have listened to that little warning voice back then of course, but this was her husband, her soul mate, the man she had envisaged growing old with. There had been little indiscretions in the early years but they had married very young and with no money and two small children she'd had no choice other than to weather those marital storms, but as the children grew so did their happiness. They worked hard and achieved a good standard of living making provision for their retirement by buying and renovating older properties which they rented out. Life was good, just unfolding in the way they had planned, until she had been caught unsuspecting and those hoped for golden years together disappeared behind a veil of pain and anguish.

She'd gone away for the weekend to get away from the oppressive atmosphere that now pervaded their home, returning to find a note scribbled on a scrap of paper telling her that he had left, ending thirty years of marriage as though cancelling an order for the milkman. She had crumpled, mentally and physically broken, unable and unwilling to get off her knees. For quite some weeks, like some wounded animal she'd taken to ground licking her wounds, finding refuge in the bottle until her grief began to turn to anger as she learnt that after discarding her like some cast off piece of wrapping paper, her husband had been parading with his new love around their old haunts like some puffed up old cockerel. Gradually, thanks in no small measure to family and friends, she'd begun to get back onto her feet again, stronger now with a steel core forged from sorrow.

She left the bathroom putting those memories behind her. She had come through the darkest of times and right now was enjoying a feeling of inner confidence that had grown from the realisation that she was coping well as an independent woman, beholden to nothing and no-one. She had become a person in her own right no longer playing second fiddle to a selfish narcissistic peacock. The phone rang and she answered it smiling to herself, "Hello Ingrid, I'm just about to leave to collect Fay, mine's a cold white wine if you get there before me."

She chuckled as she put back the handset; life was actually pretty good. She checked her hair, remembered to pick up her jacket and started down the stairs but stopped half way down. She heard a clicking sound as though someone was trying the front door, then the doorbell rang. Her heart turned over, she knew it was Keith and seeing his face distorted by the bulls' eye in the door confirmed her fears.

She'd changed the locks! He bit down on his anger, how dare she lock him out of his own house! He told himself to calm down; the last thing he wanted was a row. Life had been pretty miserable for the past few weeks. It hadn't taken long for him to realise that this new life with Marion that he had jumped into was not exactly a bed of roses. Sure the sex was great for a while but the house was dirty and always untidy and if he commented on it, she just told him to do it himself. He began to get tired of ironing his own shirts and cooking for one when something unexpected came up and she couldn't get home. She was late home more and more lately and he had begun to wonder if she was seeing someone else. How the tables had turned; now it was him being accused of jealousy and nagging.

He had begun to think more and more of the children, of Sarah and the beautiful home she had made for them. She had taken care of everything; house always clean, clothes always clean and ironed, always a full larder of good food, and he really missed her cooking. He felt ashamed when he remembered complaining on the rare occasion that she'd asked him to be home on time for a meal. He had always retorted by saying that he far preferred to eat out as then you could eat when you liked and there was always a choice of dishes, but he'd been eating out a good deal lately and what he wouldn't give for a home cooked roast. He was scared of what the future may hold. He wanted to go home, to turn the clock back. He'd been such a fool.

"Calm down, calm down just get her talking." He'd always managed to get her round to his way of thinking - if he could just explain he knew she would see sense .

Sarah went into the lounge and opened the small window adjacent to the large oak front door. "What do you want?"

"We need to talk. How are you and the kids? You look lovely by the way."

She was angry; this was the first time he had bothered with any of them since he had left – did he think her a fool. "Well, no thanks to you we are all fine. Josh and Kate are coping well with the baby, her name is Emma by the way, and he has just been promoted at work, and despite you throwing a spanner into the works Susie is doing her best to cope with her exams."

"Don't be like that love. I just want to talk. We need to sort things out – if we don't the only ones who will profit from all this are the solicitors." He was getting annoyed, "I've been such a fool – just let me in and we can sort things out."

Sarah was nonplussed. He had wrecked all their lives and now he was talking as though they had merely had a tiff. He was trying to sound contrite but the scales had fallen from her eyes and she saw him, maybe for the first time, for the self centred liar and cheat that he was.

"There's nothing to sort out. You agreed to a divorce and it's all going through. Where's horse face by the way, has she thrown you out or are you missing your creature comforts? Is that why you're really here?"

Her remarks stung him, she knew him so well. He changed tack, "Come on love. This is madness. You should think of the kids, think about what all this is doing to them. We'll all be worse off if we split – don't be so stubborn, just let's talk it through."

He was doing the usual, turning it all around onto her, using the children to pull her emotional strings but this time all it did was strengthen her resolve to press on with the divorce. She didn't want him and she certainly didn't need him. The worm had finally turned!

She shook her head amazed at his audacity and began to close the window. Now he was worried, he raised his voice, "Sarah, come on now. Be reasonable. We are all going to lose out if you don't see sense. We'll lose thousands."

Looking into his eyes she smiled and mimicking Clark Gable as best she could said "Frankly my dear, I don't give a damn," as she pulled the window to.

As she watched him march down the drive her bravado began to fade. She stood at the window watching until he was out of sight, trying to regain her composure. The phone in the hall rang, this time is was Fay. "Hi Fay, I'm just on my way. I got held up a little but I'll be round in ten." She collected keys, bag and jacket and set the alarm before closing the door to the house that had been her home for the past eighteen years.   She could not help the small tear that tickled her cheek as she walked to the garage thinking of what might have been.

Problem Neighbours

Josh let the phone ring for a few seconds before he picked up "McGiven."

"Hello Sarge, there's a Mrs Whitlock here says she wants to speak to you - can I put her through?"

Josh recognised the voice of Constable Janet Murray. "It's okay Jan – yes put her through, and any chance of a cuppa, milk no sugar and maybe the odd biscuit."

Jan tutted ,"On your bike; putting her through now."

Josh heard Ada's familiar voice asking a querulous "Hello, Sergeant McGiven please."

The Petite Chronicles

"You're through to me Ada. Are you okay?"

"Oh Josh, yes thank you Bobby and I are fine, but I would like to speak to you in private so I was wondering if you would like to call in and have dinner with us tonight, or if not tonight maybe in a day or so."

Josh's spirits lifted. Ada was a superb cook and the prospect of a home cooked meal was far more appealing than the supermarket offering that was sitting in his fridge and designated for tonight."

"As a matter of fact I am free tonight what time would suit?"

"Shall we say seven o'clock? That will give me time to walk Bobby before it gets dark."

"Seven it is, and please be careful! Don't go wandering about in the back of beyond, stick to the streets where you'll be safer."

Ada chuckled "Oh really Josh, you do fuss so. Bye bye."

Josh put down the phone wondering what that was all about. Ada wasn't the type for idle gossip so whatever she wanted to discuss must be of some importance, at least to her. He frowned slightly – he had grown very fond of her and didn't like to think that she was in any kind of trouble.

Over the past few years Josh and Ada had become firm friends and reluctantly he let his mind wander to the first time they had met. He had been investigating a series of shootings and she had been a witness to one of them, in fact she was the only witness that they had ever found. He and his colleagues had drawn a blank with their investigation having never even been close to finding a suspect, the murder weapon or any motive for the killings. None of the victims were known associates and had nothing in common save for all having abusive natures.

During the course of his investigations Josh had begun to realise that far from being the slightly confused elderly lady she purported to be, Mrs Whitlock was a keen eyed intelligent and steely woman with a military background and as he pieced together whatever meagre clues he could uncover he realised that, as crazy as it had seemed, they all lead back to her.

He thought back to the day she had realised the game was up. It was all very surreal. As they sat in her drawing room sipping tea and eating fruit scones, she had admitted her guilt but said she would deny ever having done so to anyone else, as the men she had killed were cruel and violent and she'd felt she had a duty to help their families by eliminating them. He remembered driving back to the station completely at a loss what to do. He had just taken tea with a serial killer but without her admission there was absolutely nothing to link her to the crimes and trying to get a conviction would just be a complete waste of public money, not to mention how hard all that would be on a sweet elderly lady. After a good deal of soul searching he had decided to keep things to himself and gradually wind down the investigation confident that there would be no more incidents as Ada had ditched the gun and promised that her vigilante days were over.

Josh picked up the first of the ever growing pile of files in his pending tray and flipped it open. The photo of the deceased was not a pretty sight. Her face was covered in purple bruising and the eyes and lips were swollen. Her hair was plastered to her head with blood and Josh read that she was twenty eight years old and her partner was in custody. He leant back in his chair and rubbed his chin. He was a hard working policeman who believed in the rule of law and as such had often had grave misgivings about his decision to hide the truth about Ada, but every now and again he had to admit to himself that he could see why she had been driven to take the law into her own hands.

Josh closed the file with a heavy heart. He and Ada were now inextricably linked in crime. They had perverted the course of justice and the consequences for them both would be dire. He made a mental note to ask her not to ring him at the station in future; the less anyone knew about their friendship the better.

Having timed his walk to Ada's house to perfection Josh rang her doorbell at precisely two minutes past seven. As per usual Bobby raised the alarm and could be heard skittering up and down the hall excitedly. Ada opened the door and Josh was enveloped in the gorgeous aroma of fresh bread and garlic. Greetings were enthusiastically exchanged and Josh was shown into the lounge and made comfortable with a glass of cream sherry. "Thank you Ada, now what's on your mind?"

Ada waved away his enquiry and headed off for the kitchen speaking over her shoulder, "Oh don't let's spoil our meal. I thought we could talk about it over coffee. Dinner will be ready in about fifteen minutes is that okay for you?"

Two hours later Josh and Ada sat in armchairs on either side of her fireplace which at this time of year was filled with a vase full of roses from her garden. He was feeling almost soporific after a wonderful three course meal and although he had undone the button on his trousers he still found himself reaching for a mint chocolate as he sipped his hot coffee. Reluctantly he found himself asking his hostess what she had wanted to talk about – he so wanted just to go home to bed but that would be more than churlish after having been catered for so well.

Ada sat forward wide awake and all business. "Well now, you may remember me mentioning that my neighbour Mrs Lillycroft, who lived at number sixty five, past on several months ago."

Josh nodded "Yes I do vaguely remember but...."

"It's the new owners you see. There's something very odd about the whole set up and my instincts tell me that it's odd in a bad way." Ada took a sip of her coffee before carrying on, "Poor Gillian's house had fallen into bad repair I'm afraid and I suppose I assumed that whoever took the place on would modernise it – you know, give it a bit of a facelift – but no, absolutely nothing has been done and the curtains are always closed and...."

"That's hardly a reason for suspicion is it Ada? I think Carol and I had our house for at least a couple of years before we could afford to make any improvements."

"Not on its' own I agree but the owner has a large white van that comes and goes at all hours of the night and...."

"Oh come on now Ada that means nothing at all, they could be involved in all manner of business – these days commerce runs twenty four seven and......"

"But I haven't got to the important bit. Two weeks ago I was taking Bobby for an early morning walk when he dropped his ball and it rolled underneath the van – It was parked on the road you see as Gillian didn't drive so she'd never had need to pave over her front garden. I was bending down trying to reach the ball when this brute of a man appeared and started to shout at me and the words that I did understand I wouldn't like to repeat. I tried to explain about the ball but what with him shouting me down and Bobby growling and barking I thought it prudent to just carry on with our walk and leave it behind."

"Not the nicest of neighbours I agree Ada but...."

The Petite Chronicles

"Mm,m he really was a brute of a man and foreign to boot. I would guess he is Russian or Polish from his accent – if I had taken note of all the undoubtedly rude words he called me I could probably narrow it down. Anyway, I took Bobby out for his late night walk and when I passed the van I heard a sort of wail coming from the back and then a thump as though something or someone was kicking out. There was no-one around so I took a look in the cab but it was empty. I was just about to call out when he appeared again as if from nowhere. Luckily I had another of Bobby's balls in my hand so I dropped it and let it roll so that I could pretend to be looking for it again."

"This time he pushed me against the driver's door and pulled out a knife and he made it very clear that if he caught us around his van again he would use it on Bobby. I trust Bobby's judgement you know and he absolutely hates the brute, and so do I." Ada suddenly realised what she'd said, "Oh don't worry Josh; a promise is a promise and I wouldn't dream of taking the law into my own hands ever again, but I'm as sure as eggs is eggs that there is something very wrong going on."

"Mmm he does sound a bit of a nasty sort and threatening you or anyone else with a knife is well out of order – shame there were no witnesses." Josh thought for a moment. He knew Ada well and she was no shrinking violet and maybe her instincts were sound. "There's not much I can do at the moment but I'll check with Land Registry tomorrow so that at least we know who actually owns the house."

The Petite Chronicles

"Already done it; the owner is a Mr James Lawson but the only person I've ever seen using the place is our foreign friend and if Mr Lawson is letting the property to him it must be a private arrangement as none of the local letting agents have Gillian's house on their books."

Josh shook his head and smiled "You don't let the grass grow do you Ada? I'm afraid there's not much I can do at the moment but maybe I can check out this Mr Lawson – see if he appears anywhere on our records." He checked his watch and yawned. "Thanks for a lovely evening Ada and for the lovely meal but I think I'm ready for bed."

Josh remonstrated with Ada as she walked him to the door, "Now don't go doing anything silly! Just let me see what I can find out if anything, and I'll ring in a couple of days. Promise me now that you won't antagonise your new neighbour – just let things lie – it will probably turn out that he does house clearances or something of the like."

Ada squeezed his arm "You're probably right Josh. I'll just keep my distance from now on – it would be interesting to know more about Mr Lawson though – I wonder why I've never come across him."

"Now now Ada, promise me you'll ...."

"Of course, of course I'll just watch from afar – Scouts Honour."

"Good. Thanks again my dear I'll ring soon."

Ada waved until Josh disappeared into the shadows. She closed the door and leant down to tickle Bobby. "Well I won't really be breaking a promise Bobby – after all I was never a Scout."

As was her custom Ada took Bobby out first thing before returning home after working up an appetite for breakfast. As she turned into the street she saw that there was no white van, just Bobby's blue ball lying flattened in the space that it had occupied. The temptation was just too much for Ada so after looking around to make sure the coast was clear she slipped into the overgrown front garden and made for the large bay window hoping to find a gap in the curtains, but they were tightly drawn. Bobby ran off through a hole in the side gate and Ada, worried about making too much noise calling him, pushed the rotting gate aside and followed.

It was sad to see Gillian's garden looking so forlorn. She remembered how it had been her friend's pride and joy and she would be heartbroken to see the overgrown jungle that it had become. Much to Ada's relief Bobby came hurtling out from the undergrowth, "There you are you naughty boy, come on now let's go before we get caught nosing around." As she turned to go she saw that the wooden back door, which had certainly seen better days, now had two huge shiny new bolts fixed to the outside making the old conventional Chubb lock irrelevant.

Perplexed Ada stared at these new additions as Bobby began to scratch furiously at the door. Knowing she was completely in the wrong she just could not resist slipping the bolts and trying the door. It had dropped on its' hinges a little but with a light push it opened with little resistance. The house smelled of dust and neglect and showed very little sign of occupation aside from a half used loaf and a battered saucepan perched on a camping gas ring.

Bobby raced ahead and scurried up the bare wooden stairs tail up and obviously enjoying himself. After glancing into two more rooms which were as empty and unloved as the kitchen, Ada followed Bobby up the stairs to find him scratching furiously at a door held shut with yet another bolt. Heart hammering she slid it back and pushed the door open a few inches at a time.

The stench in the room made her gag and what she saw almost made her weep. There were half a dozen mattresses on the floor and on three of them were girls who she guessed were no more than sixteen or seventeen. All had a metal anklet on one leg through which ran a heavy chain fixed to the wooden floor; the chain was just loose enough to allow the girls access to a bucket which was obviously for use as a latrine and which was the cause of the unbelievable noxious smell. All three girls appeared unconscious, induced no doubt by drugs.

"Oh Lord Bobby; I knew it; I just knew it. Let's get out of here and raise the alarm before that beast comes back."

Ada wished now that she had taken Josh's advice and updated her 'phone so that she could take a picture as evidence. She dragged a reluctant Bobby out of the room and pulled the door too sliding the bolt back into place. Scared now, she couldn't wait to get out of the house. She had stumbled on people smugglers and was under no illusion as to what would happen to her if she was caught.

Just as they reached the kitchen she heard voices and her legs turned to jelly. The only way out of the high walled garden was through the front and that way was blocked. She picked up Bobby and hid in the walk-in larder, thankful that Gillian had never got around to modernising the kitchen. She held Bobby's mouth shut and tried to breathe as quietly as she could but as the men shouted in alarm at finding the back door open Bobby struggled from her arms and began barking at the man he had taken such a dislike to.

The larder door opened to reveal a tall elegant man with a gun in his hand and a wry smile on his handsome face. "Well what have we hear? Has Goldilocks let herself in uninvited?"

Before Ada could stop herself she spoke "Mr Lawson I presume." She saw the smile disappear as the man raised the gun and brought the butt down on her head rendering her unconscious.

Lawson turned to his companion. "Shut that bloody door Gregor and shut that bloody dog up."

Gregor took a swipe at Bobby but he was too quick and ran over to his mistress frantically licking her face. In his thick accent he said "What we do now? I kill her?"

"No you fool. We'll take her with us. Get her upstairs with the others and give her a shot to keep her quiet."

"Best we kill her. She no good – no-one will pay for an old hag like that."

"Maybe, maybe not, there are some very strange people in this world Gregor so let's keep our options open – someone may be daft enough to pay a few quid for her."

Grumbling under his breath Gregor slung Ada over his shoulder and carried her upstairs followed by a very concerned Bobby. He threw her onto a mattress and kicked Bobby into the room before ramming home the bolt. The bloody old woman was trouble – he could feel it in his water.

Ada woke with a searing headache and thought she was in danger of choking – her throat was so dry and her tongue felt huge in her mouth. She realised that she was now lying on the floor of the moving van alongside her three companions with her feet tied tightly together. Bobby was pressed against her shivering. She put out a hand "It's okay Bobby, everything is okay," but everything was decidedly not okay. She became aware of the girl next to her stirring and as she awoke she began to whimper so she reached out to stroke the girl's hair in an effort to reassure her. She tried words of comfort but it was obvious the girl didn't understand.

Ada couldn't quite grasp the language spoken but was certain the poor girl came from somewhere in Eastern Europe. She tried a different tack and called out in the only other language in which she could converse "Est-ce que quelqu'un ici parle francais?"

Much to her relief a weak sounding voice replied "Oui je m'appelle Madelaine. Aidez-nous sil vous plait, aidez nous."

Ada discovered that Madelaine was from Latvia and the other two girls, Anna and Magda were from Kazakhstan and they had all opted to work in England in order to learn the language. They had gone through the same agency and had been offered jobs in London along with temporary accommodation until they could make their own way, but neither had materialised as somewhere along the line they been drugged and now found themselves in a living nightmare. All three girls had a good idea of what fate awaited them and were terrified. The van began to slow down and eventually stopped and unable to communicate verbally Ada mimed a warning to everyone to feign sleep; their guards would be less on the alert if they thought none of them had regained consciousness.

Gregor slid down from the cab and started to fill the van with diesel while James Lawson made his way to the back of the vehicle to check up on their cargo. Knowing that everyone was bound he opened one door fairly wide forgetting about the dog. Bobby was bursting to relieve himself and seeing the opportunity to do so he scooted through the gap and was gone. Gregor, coming the other way saw the dog and gave chase but of course that only made Bobby run faster – he hated that man just about as much as a dog can hate.

Lawson slammed the door shut "Oh leave the bloody thing. With a bit of luck he'll get flattened by an HGV. Inside Ada was quaking with fear for Bobby and loathing for both men. Up to now she had thought of herself as a victim but now things had changed and she was determined to make them pay for what they were doing with these girls and for what may happen to Bobby. She regretted not having her own gun any more but if she could get her hands on Lawson's she would use it without compunction; as far as she was concerned he and his loathsome companion were vermin and should be treated as such. This was a different Ada, a woman dangerously full of indignation and resolve and perfectly capable of killing.

…………………………..

Josh sat absently rubbing his chin as he scrolled through the police record of a Mr James Lawson. He was forty eight years old and had been in and out of trouble since the age of nineteen when he'd been arrested for burglary. He had recently been released from Wandsworth after serving a five year sentence for defrauding an elderly lady of her life savings. "What a charmer. Maybe Ada was on to something after all."

The phone on his desk rang and Josh picked up on the second ring. "McGiven."

"Sarge, I thought you may be interested in this, it might be just a coincidence but..."

"What's that Jan?"

"Well I remember the other day you spoke to a Mrs Whitlock, she asked especially for you, and I remember you saying that she had a little dog."

Josh was all ears now "Yes, go on."

"Well a dog was picked up near the M6 Last night just outside Wolverhampton and according to his chip he belongs to a Mrs Whitlock in Eastley Road that's just near you isn't it?"

"Yes Jan, but what about the dog?"

"Oh he's okay but we sent a car to her address this morning but there was no-one in and according to the neighbours they haven't seen Mrs Whitlock since the day before yesterday. They're a bit worried as apparently she always tells them when she's going away – it's a neighbourhood watch area and..."

"I'll be down in a jiff Jan, I just want a word with the Super but can you get someone to run me over there, I'd like to take a look." Josh hurried along to his boss muttering under his breath "Oh Ada, what the hell have you been up to now and what the hell was Bobby doing way up north?"

Having briefed his boss regarding his recent conversation with Mrs Whitlock and her concerns about her unsavoury neighbours Josh hurried downstairs and into the awaiting squad car.

As soon as the police car arrived outside Ada's, neighbours appeared and handed over her door keys. Josh and his driver, Constable Dawson let themselves in. As ever the house was clean and tidy and it was obvious from the cereal packet and unused bowl and utensils set out on the table that Ada had fully intended to return for breakfast after her usual early walk with Bobby. No-one seemed to have seen her leave the house but that was not unusual as she was an early riser.

As a routine precaution they checked through the house but Josh knew something had happened. Ada's words came flooding back to him and he truly feared for her safety. The two men left the house and made their way several doors down to number sixty five with Josh explaining as briefly as he could about the call he had received from Mrs Whitlock and her concerns about the neighbours they were going to see. Constable Dawson didn't comment but Josh was aware that the young man thought they were dealing with some crazy old lady, and in a way he couldn't blame him.

Josh knew that the house would more than likely be empty but he wanted to take a look anyway, he was worried that Ada had broken in and had maybe collapsed or had an accident or worse still had a run in with the knife man. Josh knocked on the peeling front door while Dawson went around the back. The house was deadly quiet and there was no van outside so Josh began to look for a legitimate way in. He heard Dawson calling and made his way down the side path to join him, "Look at this guv – bit strange isn't it?"

Josh looked thankfully at the two gleaming bolts "Funny business isn't it! Most people want to prevent people coming in not getting out. I think we'd better take a look inside. Keep your eyes open Constable I don't like the feel of this."

The bolts slid back smoothly and as Ada had discovered the day before the old door gave way easily with just a little push. The two men made their way silently through the kitchen and into the hall to discover the two further rooms downstairs were completely empty. Josh pointed up the stairs and both men moved as slowly and silently as was possible on the creaking wooden stairs. The contents of the main bedroom told them all they needed to know. The dirty mattresses were still spread around the floor and the chain that had held the prisoners secure was still screwed to the floorboards. Although the bucket was now empty the smell in the room was overpowering. Josh's heart sank, he was certain now that Ada was in deep trouble, that is if she was not already dead.

"We'd better radio this in Dawson. Put out an all points bulletin to keep an eye out for a white Renault Traffic van or similar last thought to be on the M6 probably heading north. We believe it to be involved in people trafficking. The occupants may have also abducted an elderly woman in her seventies and tell anyone spotting it to approach with caution. Got that?" Dawson nodded. "We'd better get someone doing door to door too. You never know, a neighbour may have seen something."

"Okay guv; on my way."

....

The van set off once again and Ada was distraught with the loss of Bobby and she was so worried for him. She was also feeling pretty dreadful. Her head was pounding and not having had anything to eat or drink at all for goodness knows how long, she felt really light headed. Unable to do much else the captives lay listening to the noise of tyres on the road as the van ate up mile after mile taking them further and further from help. After what must have been several hours they felt the van turn and slow down; the fear they all felt now was palpable.

Eventually after a few more twists and turns they came to a halt, the doors swung open and after having their hands bound Ada and the girls were dragged from the van unable to shield their eyes from the stark fluorescent lighting which was blinding them after being in complete darkness for hours. The van had been driven into some vast warehouse and close up to a small room partitioned off in a corner of the huge space, obviously used at some time as an office. With hands and feet bound they had no way of protecting themselves as they were hauled into the room landing heavily as they were dumped unceremoniously on the cold concrete floor.

Lawson spoke, "There we are ladies. Not long now and you will all be on your separate ways."

Ada was fuming "Oh for pity's sake! The poor girls are in a dreadful state. Have you no humanity in you man?"

Her captor looked slightly taken aback – good, he was on the defensive. "The very least you could do is untie our feet and let us move about, and if you had any sense you'd get us something to drink – people die of dehydration you know and these young things will be no good to you dead."

Still smarting from Ada's words, Lawson vented his anger by shouting orders at Gregor to cut some of the prisoner's ropes and fetch water and biscuits from the van, "And fetch a bucket too, we don't want piss all over the floor." If looks could kill Lawson would be dead but Gregor did as he was told albeit reluctantly and with ill grace.

After half an hour Ada and the girls began to feel a little better. They had suffered badly with pins and needles when they first stood and tried walking on dead legs but the meagre nourishment had helped to fortify them so that they were able to assess their undoubtedly dire situation. Ada was deep in thought weighing up the odds against making a break when Anna shuffled over to join her sitting on the floor where they could not be seen through the waist high windows. Although they couldn't communicate that well they had managed a little with sign language and now Anna nudged her arm and smiled. She held up her hands which were tied palms together and Ada watched fascinated as the girl somehow managed to dislocate the fingers and thumb on one hand enabling her to slip it through the rope. Once free she set about loosening the bonds of the others so that they still looked secure but now were loose enough to slip off.

The girls' were all smiles at this little victory and Ada wondered at the exuberance of youth even under the most difficult of circumstances. Yes, they were now free of their bonds but how to get the better of the two morons outside. She had racked her brains for some sort of escape plan and the only one she could come up with involved Madelaine. She was reluctant to use the girl but she had striking looks and men will always be men, so Ada asked if she would be willing to distract Lawson in the age old way in the hope that he could be put off his guard long enough for them to get hold of his gun. It was risky and not much of a plan, but that was all they had.

The Petite Chronicles

Ada was full of admiration for the girl who didn't hesitate to agree to do what she could; they didn't have to wait long. At the sound of bolts being drawn on the office door Madelaine pulled up her skirt to display far more of her long slim legs than she was really comfortable with, but needs must. Lawson came into the room and she at once became coquettish and slid her legs one against the other as suggestively as she could. Lawson walked in carrying a bottle of water but his eyes went immediately to the girl, as was intended. Madelaine spoke to him in French and her meaning was clear in any language.

Ada took up her part "Well, what a shameless little hussy!

Never taking his eyes from the girl's legs Lawson spoke "What she say then?"

"She's disgusting. She says she will swap a favour to you in exchange for food for all of us. I suppose I should be grateful, but I just don't know what the world is coming to. Young girl's these days need a good spanking if you ask me and…."

Lawson leered "That isn't a bad idea." He thrust the water at Ada "I don't know about feeding you lot but I'm going to get my fill of this little lady and she looks like she's up for it too."

Lawson bent over the girl and started to yank her to her feet, "I'll just take her somewhere a little more private and…"

Madelaine sunk her teeth into his hand and Ada, Anna and Magda were on him. Caught completely unaware he fell to his knees shouting and cursing, throwing and landing punches while the girls scratched kicked and bit him in turn. Somehow in the melee Ada managed to slip her hand into his pocket and felt the comfort of hard steel beneath her fingers. She grabbed the barrel and clubbed Lawson, who it had to be said, although outnumbered was in danger of winning the fight. He fell silently to the ground clutching his head with blood pouring between his fingers.

Alerted by all the noise Gregor appeared in the doorway gun in hand and face like thunder. He took a step towards Ada; he'd wanted to kill the old lady from the beginning, she was trouble and these girls needed teaching a lesson so he would give them one that they wouldn't forget. He took aim "Now I kill ……" but before he could finish his sentence he fell to the ground screaming out in pain and shock when he saw that his knee was now just a shattered bloody mess. Disbelieving, he looked up to see the old lady take aim once again and he flung out his arms entreating her not to shoot. She seemed to consider her options for what felt to him an eternity but at last she lowered the gun and he began to cry – not tears of gratitude but of anger and frustration at his impotence as she picked up his gun and handed it to Madelaine. The sound of the gunfire in such a confined space made everyone's ears ring and quite some minutes past before everyone was able to absorb what had just taken place.

The Petite Chronicles

Under Ada's instruction the girls dragged a whimpering Gregor to lie alongside a confused Lawson and took the phones from both men. Using the ropes that had once tied them; they bound the two with their arms behind their backs and bolted them securely in the very room that had so recently been their prison, all immune to Gregor's entreaties for help which fell on deaf ears.

Once outside in the relative safety of the warehouse they huddled together shocked, bloody and bruised but safe. Ada was the first to return to some sort of normality and realised that they were not out of the woods yet. This place had been arranged as a rendezvous point and whoever was coming could turn up at any moment. Urging the others to follow her despite hurting from head to foot, she made her way out into the night. A small group of women, smarting from their wounds, but overwhelmingly happy that they had escaped a fate that none of them wanted to think about.

Once out of the Industrial Estate and onto a main road they managed to flag down a taxi, but not before half a dozen vehicles had slowed then moved on at the sight of the ragged blood stained group at the side of the road. The owner of the cab Georgio Papadopoulos had been listening in on the police radio frequency and so was well aware of the white van alert and it was fresh in his mind when he saw the sorry looking group, putting two and two together when he saw amongst them a white haired elderly lady.

He'd stumbled right into a real police drama – just wait until he got home to tell the family.

Georgio, contacted the police and drove his passengers to the nearest motorway service station as agreed where they were met with half a dozen police cars and two ambulances. Ada, with a little help from Georgio, was able to tell where they had been held and described the warehouse as best she could, explaining that there were two injured men still in the building – one with a bullet wound. In a trice two cars sped off followed by one of the ambulances, all with sirens blaring.

....

Several days later Josh was sipping coffee in Ada's living room. "Well I've got to hand it to you Mrs. Whitlock you certainly do have a nose for trouble. Do you realise what kind of danger you were in – what kind of people you were dealing with?"

"I'm afraid I do Josh and I must admit it was very tempting to finish off that brute of a man after what he did to Bobby, but I didn't did I? I think you should give me a few brownie points for that."

Josh shook his head – she was incorrigible. "I don't know what's going to become of all this Ada but thanks to you we've got leads to the whole trafficking network. It's a massive operation and our compatriots are just about to spring the trap throughout Europe."

"Good, good. Now, have a piece of cake Josh, I put fresh cream in it especially for you."

Josh sunk his teeth into the delicious cake. He would never be able to fathom this woman who was so full of contradictions, but what the hell – she was a marvellous cook.

My Girl

Tamsin turned off the lane and onto the cart track that lead to her sister's farm. Her small low slung Mazda was not the most suitable vehicle for tackling the rough deeply rutted track and the last thing she wanted was to damage the cars sump or silencer.

Memories came flooding back as she ground her way along the half mile track She was the youngest of three children. Her brother Robert, who had sadly died ten years ago, had been the eldest, Mary was two years his junior and then, very much as a surprise, Tamsin had appeared eight years later. She shook her head ruefully – what a name to be saddled with! It sounded like the name some glamour model would adopt. She could only surmise that as she had arrived just after her parents purchased their first house mother must have

had delusions of grandeur and ordinary names like those of her siblings just wouldn't do.

She spoke to the little dog who sat beside her strapped into his baby seat "Not long now Rhett, I can see the house from here." They had an amazing rapport and the little terrier seemed to nod his head in understanding. She had always wanted a dog but being single and living and working in London it had never really been possible so when she had retired eighteen months ago she had been determined to find herself a little companion and that is how Rhett had come into her life. She had fallen in love with him as soon as she'd seen him at the rescue centre. He was a smart little dog both in looks and guile and they had

connected immediately. His wiry fur was black and white though his face was all white save for a thin black line around his mouth that looked for all the world like a pencilled on moustache and which turned up slightly at each end making him look decidedly rakish.

As a young girl Tamsin had taken herself to the local cinema, which was accurately nicknamed the flea pit. The odd flea was the price you had to pay for an afternoon's entertainment but in her eyes it was

worth it, especially on the afternoon they had screened
Gone with the Wind. She had been entranced by the film and had immediately formed an enormous crush on the dashing moustachioed Rhett Butler which made it easy for her when it came to choosing a name for her new little friend.

Tamsin had been fairly academic as a child and unlike her siblings had been awarded a place at grammar school which unfortunately, didn't go down too well with her parents as it meant them having to pay out for bus fares and all the other paraphernalia that had been unnecessary for Robert and Mary. University had been out of the question so when she had finished school she managed to get a job with the local newspaper, initially as a general assistant and then as a junior journalist covering weddings, funerals and all the usual events that were attended by minor dignitaries.

It was at one of these events that she had met Tom. He was a trainee vet and as with Rhett she had known he was for her in an instant. Before long, much to her mother's disapproval, they had found a flat and were living blissfully happy together. Tamsin smiled to herself as she remembered those times. It was the tail end of the swinging sixties and they had enjoyed life to the full, but it all came to a shattering end when Tom had been killed in a motoring accident on his way to a call out.

Unable to live with memories which were all around her she had moved to London where she'd been lucky enough to be taken on by a leading newspaper. The only way she could deal with her grief was to throw herself into her work and it was not long before she
became a valued member of staff. She seemed to have a nose for news and over her career had earned an enviable reputation as an investigative journalist.

Eventually she had started out on new relationships but each one fizzled out as none of the men that had come into her life were a match for Tom. She had tried to fill her emptiness by living a wild life and burning the candle at both ends but eventually, in her mid forties, she had decided that she didn't need another half and quite liked being independent and free. She just didn't want to compromise or have anyone trying to influence her life. She had a busy lifestyle with the work that she loved taking up most of it. She had some good friends and she'd found a sort of contentment in realising that although there would never be another Tom she had a happy and fulfilling life and the nature of her work reminded her every day that she was one of the lucky ones.

As she pulled into the yard Mary ran out to meet her accompanied by her two border collies. With her pepper and salt hair piled on top of her head she was the farmer's wife to perfection; slightly plump with pink shiny cheeks and beautiful skin that belied her years.

She had on a loose fitting woollen dress which was largely covered by a flour dusted pinafore. As Tamsin climbed out of her car Mary flung her arms around the sister she hadn't seen for several years. "Oh Tammy, I'm so glad you could come." They hugged each other
both too emotional to speak.

Rhett had been observing things from his seat. He saw competition in the two dogs outside – better be on his best behaviour. After all he was used now to being the centre of attention and that was the way he liked it. Mary bent to look at him through the window "Oh Tammy, what a lovely little dog, he looks like he's got a taches and he's smiling doesn't he?" But before Tamsin could comment, Mary clasped her hands to her face "He winked at me! I swear he just winked at me!"
Once the dogs had checked each other out and no fur went flying Tamsin collected her case from the boot and followed Mary indoors. The kitchen was warm and there were beautiful smells coming from the Aga. The slab on the big wooden table was strewn with flour and the remnants of left over pastry, most of which was now cooking and smelling so delicious.
"Let's have a nice hot drink then I'll clear up this mess and you can unpack. Oh I'm so happy you'll be here

for Christmas" She laughed "Although I'm not sure how glad you'll be when all the tribe are here."

They took their coffee into the parlour as Mary called it and Tamsin could not help but comment on how beautiful it was. There was a huge Christmas tree in one corner and each ceiling beam was festooned with shiny hanging decorations that glittered in the light thrown from the fire glowing in the inglenook.

As she sank down into the huge soft sofa Tamsin couldn't stop the pang of pain and sadness that overwhelmed her – this is what she and Tom had imagined – "Oh Tom, I miss you so!"

As ever Rhett came to her rescue and changed her mood when he bounded in followed by Sukie and Madge – it seemed he'd sorted out the pecking order and the girls were happy to oblige. All three settled on their rug covered old settee and the two sisters settled down to catch up on the parts of each other's lives missed since they last met.

**

The few days leading up to the main event were a magical time for both women. Ben, Mary's husband of nearly fifty years, disappeared at first light only popping in for the odd cup of tea to warm him up so their time together was uninterrupted. They baked, wrapped presents and prepared vegetables talking non-stop all the while. They popped into town to pick up last minute bits, and despite Mary's protestations Tamsin bought a couple of cases of expensive wine before settling down to enjoy an indulgent cream tea, while the sounds of Christmas Carollers singing in the town square drifted over them.

Mary's tribe, which consisted of her three daughters their husbands and eight grand children, turned Christmas Day into one of the happiest and most memorable times that Tamsin could remember. Mary was a superb cook so Christmas lunch was something to behold and be savoured, then it was an afternoon walk for everyone while Mary and Ben had a well deserved snooze before games were played and the table was once again spread with food.

Boxing day was set to be a repeat performance but it was overshadowed by some unwelcome news. Tamsin and Mary were chatting in the kitchen when the 'phone rang. Tamsin, who was beating eggs and cream for the quiches, stopped to listen when her sister's cheery tone suddenly changed – something was wrong. She waited for Mary who returned white faced – she had obviously had some bad news. Tamsin waited for her to speak "That was my Gillian. They won't be coming today; Joe's sister has been found dead – they say she's committed suicide!" She sat shaking her head "Poor Joe is in a bad way. It can't be true. Just can't be - why would she?"

They did what they could to resurrect the day but no-one was in the mood for celebration, that is with the exception of Rhett, Sukie and Madge who found that the five grand children that were present were a constant source of food – in the words of a past elder statesman "They had never had it so good."

**

The next day Tamsin, in the absence of Ben who was the most kindly soul but who avoided emotional situations, accompanied her sister to Gillian's house. Her husband Joe was grief stricken and in bed having succumbed to the strong sedative administered by his doctor. He and his sister Gemma had lost both parents in their teens and were therefore very close, so
losing her was a tremendous blow, especially when it seemed she had left him deliberately.

As she ushered them in it was obvious that Gillian had been crying but she was angry too. "How could she do such a thing? And at Christmas time too! Why would she? They were only here a couple of weeks or so ago when she brought the kid's presents round and she
seemed fine - happy even."

The Petite Chronicles

After a couple of hours comforting Gillian and her children as best they could, the sisters said their goodbyes and sat in silence as they chugged along in Mary's old Jeep. Tammy broke the silence, "Gillian said they called round, who was Gemma with then?"

"Oh, she was with her husband Nial; he's some sort of musician – plays in a rock band so I gather. Joe wasn't that keen on him but she'd already had two failed marriages and the lad seemed to make her happy so the rest of us accepted him – sort of." She screwed up her face as though wondering whether she should say any more, "He was quite a bit younger than her and to be honest I thought she was a fool but it wasn't my place to pass comment, but you have to wonder if it was her or her money that attracted him in the first place. I suppose when I think of it she hasn't looked like her old self for a while. I mean, maybe he
wasn't as good for her as we all thought, otherwise why would she do such a thing."

Tamsin's journalistic instincts kicked in "So she had money then; and your Joe seems to have done well for himself as well."

"Yes, well by the time their parents were killed they had built up a large property portfolio which of course Joe and Gemma inherited. I think they both sold a little of their stock to buy their own properties

but they still have very healthy incomes from rentals and I know
Joe is still investing in new stock as he calls it. Of course we've never asked questions but I don't think money has ever been a problem for either of them."

When at work Tamsin's mantra whenever her suspicions were aroused was – 'follow the money' and now she smelled a rat. "I'd be very interested to meet this Nial. Will you be paying him a visit at all?"

Mary gave her sister a knowing smile, "I suppose I should call on him to convey my condolences; I'll ring him when I get home and ask if I can pop in tomorrow – we've got plenty of cold meat and such so I could pack him something to tide him over the next few
days. I've never heard mention of any family on his side so the poor lad could be stuck there in that big house all on his own and..."

Tammy put a hand on her sister's arm; Mary was kindness personified but she was inclined to collect lame ducks even if they didn't realise they needed rescuing. "Hold your horses sis, just see how he is when you telephone him."

Mary frowned then nodded in agreement. It was a few minutes before she spoke again, almost to herself "Seriously though Gemma was a lovely young woman and it's just tragic that she's gone from all of us."

The next morning found Mary bustling around in the kitchen. The 'few things' she had packed for Nial were bursting from the top of an ancient shopping trolley. Tammy cleared away the breakfast dishes and once Ben had been seen off to work with his lunch box filled
with Christmas goodies, the sisters set off to meet Nial as arranged by Mary the night before.

Mary's old Jeep looked slightly out of place as they pulled up on the circular gravel drive. Wisteria Lodge was a mock Tudor creation and the skeleton of bare sinewy branches that crept along large parts of the lower wall left one in no doubt as to how the building had acquired its name. As they stepped onto the gravel they were surprised to be greeted by the sound of loud rock music belting out of an open bedroom window.

They stood outside for a full five minutes before at last the music stopped and the doorbell could be heard by
Nial who then came out to greet them.

Tammy knew that Gemma's husband was younger than her but nonetheless she was surprised when she saw him. Gemma had been in her late forties but this man looked not much more than a boy. He was slim, almost puny and his dark hair hung from a centre parting almost down to his neck. Before he could say anything Mary, ever the earth mother, had gathered him up into her arms and almost carried him indoors leaving Tammy to drag in the trolley. They went into the kitchen where Mary took charge and put on a kettle to make tea.

In just a few minutes all three were sat around the kitchen table. Nial accepted their condolences with a wan smile and for a few moments there was an awkward silence before he cleared his throat and started to talk about his wife. Of course, her suicide had been a bolt from the blue – it had come as much as a shock to him as everyone else. It seemed that there had been some tension between them ever since Mary had invited them for Christmas Day. He had wanted to take up the offer but they'd argued about it as Gemma had insisted that they stay at home. She'd wanted just the two of them to have a quiet day
together.

Nial wrung his hands as tears began to fall "We were both so stubborn and it got out of hand; we even ended up sleeping in separate rooms!"

Mary jumped up from her seat and tore off a strip of kitchen roll "Oh my dear, the last thing we wanted to do was upset you."

Nial patted his face and blew his nose "No, no. honestly, it's good to have someone to talk to. I've been going over and over it all in my head and it's my fault you see – all my fault."

There was a pause before he carried on "Because we weren't talking it was all a bit of a mess so when Christmas Eve came I asked Gemma if she would come shopping with me as we had absolutely nothing in," he paused throwing back his head and sighing, "But she just ran upstairs and slammed the bedroom door," he paused again seemingly finding it difficult to speak, "So I shouted at her. I said she'd ruined Christmas and I hated her." Fighting back more tears he carried on "I stormed out and went to the pub to get drunk." He sank his face into his folded arms wailing "Oh God, if only I'd come home!"

Mary now close to tears herself, leant across the table and stroked his head while trying to offer words of comfort. There was little Tammy could do and unlike Mary, she had been underwhelmed by Nial's performance. She had interviewed many grieving relatives in her time and prided herself on being able to differentiate between the crocodile tears she had just witnessed and real grief.

The mood in the kitchen was instantly dispelled when the door bell rang. As Nial was still being comforted by Mary ,Tammy opened the door to find two soberly dressed men who she instantly recognised as policemen. The younger of the two was she guessed in his mid forties and the older man twenty years or so his senior, and both she thought were rather good looking.

She showed them into the kitchen where Nial and Mary still sat at the table. Nial stood and glared at the younger man "Not you again! What do you want this time? I can't tell you any more than I already have – why can't you just leave me alone?"

The younger man looked at the two sisters "If you wouldn't mind ladies, we just wanted a word with Mr O'Connor."

Mary led the way into the sumptuously furnished sitting room where they waited for the police to finish their business mostly in silence. Tammy was thoughtful; had she imagined it or had she seen a flicker of fear in Nial's eyes when he saw the detective. She got up and wandered around the room.

Apart from a portrait of an attractive young woman, whom she assumed to be Gemma, there were no pictures of the happy couple anywhere. She sank down into a settee and noticed a small gilt picture frame which lay face down on the walnut occasional table in front of her, left as though in a hurry as the back had not yet been fitted in place. She turned it over and there smiling out at her was Nial standing proudly at the bow of what looked to be a small yacht named 'My Girl'.

They waited until the police had gone so that they could say their goodbyes before leaving, but then only after Mary had extracted a promise from the grieving widower that he would ring whenever he needed anything. On the way home Tammy couldn't help but
ask if the couple had owned a boat "Heavens no! The last thing Gemma would ever want is to go anywhere near a boat, let alone own one. That's how her parents died you see. They were killed in a boating accident – here one day, gone the next."

Mary was overjoyed when Tammy asked if she could stay on until the New Year. She explained that she had half promised to visit a friend who lived in Brighton over the holiday and as the farm was considerably nearer to Brighton than her own home in London it would make sense to go from there. She would only be gone overnight and when she returned they could see the New Year in together and make a real holiday of it.

**

The next morning Ben was sent off with his packed lunch as usual and Tammy and Rhett set off for Brighton with a basket full of food that Mary had insisted they take 'just in case' but of course Tammy was not going to visit a friend, she was going in

search of 'My Girl'. She had that familiar itch that told her things were not what they seemed and she just had to
scratch it.

She headed for Brighton where she checked out the harbour without any luck. Then on to Chichester but no luck there either. By now, although early evening, it was cold and dark and the twinkling Christmas lights that shone from almost every house that she passed
made her feel lonely and a little vulnerable. She had never really given any thought to homeless people up to now, but this must be what it was like – watching the warm cosy world go by while you had no part in it.

She put out a hand to stroke Rhett's head – thank goodness she had him with her; time to find somewhere to stay. It took at least ten phone calls before she found anywhere that would accept her and a dog. Although it proved to be a little shabby the B & B was on the main road and relatively easy to find.

She was shown into a small room on the first floor and hooray, it had an en suite. Within fifteen minutes she had showered and spread out Mary's picnic. Bless her; she had even put in food, water and a bowl for Rhett and one of the half bottles of Sauvignon Blanc that she kept in for carol singers. She found a film on the television and lay back in bed with Rhett snuggled up against her, both completely full and relaxed. The only thing that troubled her as she drifted off into sleep was the thought of those poor homeless souls who were still outside in the cold.

The next morning Tamsin and Rhett set off for Southampton, she wasn't sure what she would do if she struck out again but there was no point in thinking about that now. The town was busy with shoppers scurrying from sale to sale resembling a swarm of multi
coloured bees. Eventually she found a parking space close to the harbour and with Rhett on his lead they set off at a brisk walk.

She hadn't gone far when she heard someone calling her name; she turned in the direction of the voice and was surprised to see the older of the two men she had seen yesterday at Wisteria Lodge. He smiled "I'm sorry for calling out, but it is Miss Tremain isn't it?"

He put out his hand as he approached "I'm Geoff Walker; I was up at the house yesterday with a colleague." He shook her hand vigorously "I can see I've caught you by surprise. Do you fancy grabbing a hot drink somewhere – we need to talk."

Tamsin was non-plussed, this was the very last thing she had expected to happen. Geoff pointed to a café up ahead "I expect we'll have to sit outside as we have the dog – are you okay with that?" Tamsin could think of nothing to say so just nodded in agreement.

As it happened the café was empty so there was no objection to Rhett being inside. Over a cup of hot chocolate Tamsin learned that Geoff had worked with the Met police until he retired several years ago but on the odd occasion, budget allowing, he did the odd bit on a consultancy basis hence his showing up yesterday with Detective Sergeant Richards who wanted his opinion on the case.
On the face of it they were dealing with a simple suicide, but Richards wasn't happy with the husband's story and wanted to dig deeper.

He had recognised Tamsin immediately as her picture had often appeared in the papers and on television and apparently, Geoff's old governor had a high regard for her "He used to say you were the human equivalent of a bloodhound. He meant it as a compliment but I must say you are much, much too attractive for such a comparison."

Tamsin blushed and attempted to hide behind her mug. "So why are you here in Southampton?"

"I'm guessing you saw the photo too. Richards asked him about the boat but he said it was just a holiday snap that Gemma had taken, but we know she hated boats and the water and wouldn't go anywhere near either so, being the old bloodhound that I am."

"You thought you'd come looking for 'My Girl'."

"That's about it." He picked up the mugs and returned them to the counter. "So, shall we go hunting?"

"Yes but what exactly is Nial's version of events over Christmas Eve and Christmas Day?

"The lad says he went to the pub in a huff and got blind drunk and doesn't remember much until waking up in his car outside the pub and driving home in the early hours. He crashed out in bed and didn't wake up until late afternoon and it wasn't until then that he thought he would try to make it up with his wife but he couldn't find her until he eventually looked in her bedroom. He was still hung over and really shaken up so he dialled 999."

Geoff opened the door and stepped aside for Tamsin and Rhett to pass through, "The landlord at the pub confirmed that he was pretty drunk and stayed until closing time but he can't say either way about him being asleep in the car park. He said there were several cars left there overnight but they were all gone by opening time next day."

The Petite Chronicles

With Rhett stepping out jauntily beside them they walked arm in arm heading for the harbour, heads down against the chill wind that had sprung up. They struck gold pretty quickly. 'My Girl' was moored between two much larger yachts but there was no mistaking her.

As they stood taking photographs a voice hailed them from above. "He's not around. Do you want to come in for a brew, it's freezing out here." They didn't need asking twice, it was indeed freezing but here was someone who could hopefully solve the small riddle of
Nial's photograph.

The cabin was warm and cosy and something delicious was cooking in the oven. "The name's Johnny – Johnny Small. " He laughed at the obvious joke as he was at least six foot three and obviously worked out. "If you're looking for Denny I can't help you. He comes
and goes you know – we're like ships that pass in the night." He smiled broadly at another of his own jokes.

The two explained that they were friends of Denny and hoped they would find him here as he said he would be around over Christmas. They learned that Denny would often pop down for a couple of days on his own but his wife only ever came at weekends as she
worked.

Johnny was a good host and obviously didn't get to see too many people as before they could refuse he was laying a table for three. The tot of brandy he had laced their coffee with had been very welcome and they were feeling pretty relaxed so when he more or less told them they were staying for lunch they just shrugged at each other – this was not turning out to be such a bad day.

Over the course of lunch they learnt quite a bit about Johnny but more interestingly they learnt from a succession of photos they were shown that Denny was in fact Nial and his 'wife' Michelle was an attractive blonde who worked as a fitness trainer, a fact that was
obvious from the many pictures they were shown.

Pleased with the way the day had gone they eluctantly stepped out in the cold afternoon which was already losing light. As he tucked a couple of incriminating photos into his pocket Geoff linked arms with Tamsin, and it felt so right. "Well, we've got the little beggar
now so I suggest we find somewhere to stay tonight and then check out our Michelle tomorrow unless you've got any other ideas. I passed a pub on the way into town and they were advertising rooms and we could sneak Rhett in if we have to - what do you say?"

It made sense to Tamsin so she agreed to drive as Geoff's car was safe in a twenty four hour car park. Before long they were in The King's Head listing the fitness centres they would be visiting tomorrow. There were plenty of rooms available and dogs were welcome so they ordered dinner and agreed to meet downstairs in the cosy bar once they had freshened up
and she had 'phoned Mary to let her know that she was staying one more night with her fictitious friend.

**

Tamsin hadn't enjoyed herself since she couldn't remember when. Geoff was such good company and she had to admit to herself that she was actually very attracted to a man for the first time since losing Tom.

Geoff's story more or less paralleled her own. He had been happily married long enough to have two daughters but his wife had died when they were young and for him there had never been anyone else. "So when I retired I found the country cottage we had always dreamed of; you know, log fire, beams and leaded window, thatched roof. I know it sounds silly but I wanted to find it for her and…"

Tamsin reached out and put her hand over his. She knew exactly what he meant. Her eyes filled as she remembered how she and Tom had pictured themselves in just such a setting.

The Petite Chronicles

She smiled at him as tears rolled down her cheeks as Rhett pushed his head between her knees. He was sensing he was getting left out of things here and that wouldn't do.

Next morning all three enjoyed a hearty breakfast as Rhett had charmed the landlady into giving him his own dish of sausages. When they entered the third gym they couldn't believe their luck – there she was blond hair piled above a very pretty face. The name on her badge was Stephanie but there was no mistaking that this was Nial's erstwhile wife. After a brief
conversation she agreed to meet them in the coffee shop across the road when her stint at the desk finished in ten minutes.

She was all gushing smiles when they mentioned Denny but all attempts at pleasantries were abandoned when it became clear to her that they had
been found out.

It was soon obvious however that Nial had been playing games with her too. She had gone
along with the false names because as soon as his divorce was through Nial had promised to marry her. As far as she was concerned poor Nial was getting a very raw deal so they had to keep the boat a secret from his wife who was already set to take half of his

business and his home even though she had never worked or helped him to make his money.

Although Stephanie had been blessed with beauty she was somewhat lacking in the cerebral department and Tamsin could not help but feel sorry for the girl as the scales fell from her eyes.

At first she was angry and defended Nial but somewhere deep inside she had always known things didn't add up and she began to ask questions. The anger she had first directed at them grew as she learned just how many lies she had been told but the anger turned to fear when she heard that Gemma's death, which had come as a shock to her, was being investigated as suspicious and it was at that point she told them about her Gran's pills.

Stephanie had moved in with her Gran two years ago when she began work at the gym. It was convenient for both of them as she lived rent free and Gran had someone to look out for her, but within six months her Gran had died and it was only when clearing up her things that she had found stacks of pain killers and sleeping pills that had been prescribed for the old lady but which she had hardly ever taken.

She had meant to hand them in but never got around to it until a few weeks ago when she'd bagged them all up in readiness to take to the chemist, but that day Nial happened to say he had a headache so she took out a pack of painkillers for him and when he saw how many pills there were he said he would drop them off for her as they shouldn't be left lying around, but she remembered him cracking a joke about giving them to the wife and saving on an expensive divorce.

Both Tamsin and Geoff were satisfied that the poor girl was as much a victim in the whole sorry tale as Gemma. They left her with assurances that she was not in any trouble and made their way back to Geoff's car.

He had a good deal to report to his colleague and Tamsin had to face her sister and admit that she had lied about going to a friend; she also had to break the news that Nial was a cheat and a fraud at the very least and she knew how much that would hurt her kind hearted and trusting sister.

As Geoff approached his car her heart sank a little, she had enjoyed being with him and now he was going. He turned back abruptly and tapped on Rhett's window. Tamsin lowered it and he leaned in patting Rhett on the head. "I was wondering if I could take you out to dinner sometime, that is if the other man in your life here, wouldn't mind."

She was flustered but managed to blurt out "Oh I'm sure he wouldn't object."

The Petite Chronicles

As Geoff slipped into his car she drove slowly past and gave him a wave. Her heart was fluttering in her chest as she headed for home buoyed up with the knowledge that they would meet again.

The light was fading as she approached the farmhouse. Sukie and Madge came bounding out to meet Rhett and they scurried off into the dark as Tamsin opened the kitchen door. Ben sat rosy cheeked supping a pint of Christmas ale as Mary served up a plate of meat and potato pie.

Tamsin sat down "I'm afraid I've a confession to make to you." She told them where she had been and why and what she had discovered.

Ben rubbed his chin "So that poor girl picked another wrong un. Happen she was just too proud to tell us all – couldn't face no more."

Mary was obviously upset "Better see our Joe in the morning – only fair he knows about that no good."

Two nights later Tamsin was sitting opposite Geoff in a gastro pub sipping Sauvignon Blanc and being brought up to date with events. It seemed that once wheels had been set in motion it hadn't taken long to uncover the extent to which Nial had been cheating his wife.

The Petite Chronicles

Gemma had been trusting and let him handle their domestic affairs, so she was unaware that he had forged her signature on several hire purchase agreements including one for the boat and had been steadily transferring money from her account into a second one in his name. She had given him a fairly generous allowance so never queried how he could afford all the expensive guitars and sound equipment that flooded into their home, especially when she thought he was earning his own money at gigs which in truth were just a cover for his weekends away.

Mary sighed, "What a mess, and what about the pills?"

"Well she was full of them. I don't see that there is any way of proving he actually killed her but you can bet your life he made sure she knew they were there. My theory is that he taunted her behind closed doors and made her life an absolute misery - probably said he
was leaving her. He kept her away from her family and purposely left her alone, so on Christmas Day who knows what went on! All I know is that I hope they throw the book at him."

They finished their meal and walked out into a perfect crisp moonlit night. Geoff turned and kissed her "I was wondering if you would like to try out my cottage for size – see if it matches up to your expectations."

Tamsin's heart missed a beat "I would like that very much, but what about Rhett?"

"Oh I'll ring him when we get to mine; I'm sure he won't mind you being away for one night."

They walked arm in arm to Geoff's car. "He winked at me you know. When I came to pick you up – I swear that darned dog winked at me."

<u>Percychatteybooks</u>
Story Telling (R)
Somerset House
6070 Birmingham Business Park
Birmingham
B37 7BF
Registered Number 2299335

Produced and published in the Hondon Valley,
Southern Spain